PRAISE FOR
CURSE OF THE KO
90% HUMAN

Curse of the Komodo is the ultimate field trip nightmare... and young readers will be most entertained.

Diana Perry
Story Monsters Ink magazine review
November 2018 issue

Curse of the Komodo is a fun read for young adult readers as well as adults! Filled with animal facts and a spell-binding story, this book hooks readers from start to finish!

L. Burnham
Teacher, Toledo, Ohio

I read *90% Human* straight through! It's a winner. My granddaughter, a huge Komodo fan who loved the first one, is going to love this one. She had her first summer sleepover camp this summer and will really "get" the setting.

Deanna K Klingel
Author of "Rebecca & Heart"

I found much excitement, adventure, danger and several delightful mysteries to solve in this book. Young readers will love how the mysteries unravel, and parents will find *90% Human* a great way to get their kids to read more. I couldn't put it down.

Diana Perry
Story Monsters Ink magazine review
February 2019 issue

Return to Komodo Island

Return to Komodo Island

M.C. Berkhousen

Illustrations by Kalpart

Progressive
RISING PHOENIX PRESS ®

Published 2019 by Progressive Rising Phoenix Press, LLC
www.progressiverisingphoenix.com

ISBN: 978-1-950560-08-0

Printed in the U.S.A.
1st Printing

Edited by Carol Gaskin

Front Cover illustration by Kalpart

Book Cover and Interior Design by William Speir
Visit: http://www.williamspeir.com

For my children,
Amy, Jennifer, and David
With Love

Acknowledgements

It takes a lot of people to get a book from the author to the reading public. Thank you Amanda Thrasher and the publishing team at Progressive Rising Phoenix Press for your help in publishing this book.

Thanks also to my supportive and helpful editor, Carol Gaskin, for polishing the manuscript and making it the best it could be.

A special thanks to Jennifer Muse, Pamela Kelso, and Elizabeth Holland for taking the time to read the manuscript and provide helpful feedback. Thanks also to my critique group; Pamela Kelso, Judith Scharren, Joette Rozanski, Charles Abood and Elizabeth Holland, for providing feedback and suggestions throughout the development of the manuscript.

My heartfelt thanks to the people who live and work on Komodo Island and I ask for your patience regarding any inaccuracies. Though I've done extensive research about your beautiful island, I have created characters and places that do not exist in order to tell a story.

Last, I'd like to thank the most important group, my readers! You are the reason I write.

M.C.

Komodo Island

The Gili's

ferry to Bali

LEMBAR

Ranger S

Table of Contents

The Psychology of Jake 1

The Passenger from China 23

Once a Rat, Always a Rat............................. 44

Shipwreck... 59

Rescue... 74

The Medicine Woman's Daughter...................... 83

The Hole in the Whole 98

Nemesis..114

Mairghread and Roux.................................128

Outnumbered 143

What is in the One is in the Whole...................158

Saving Roux 169

One Last Thing About the Curse...................181

The Last Task..195

Epilogue 206

Family Tree

Dunn (m. Katerie, medicine woman's daughter)

Angelina

Katerie and Dunn divorce. Dunn marries Helen.

Dunn & Katerie   Dunn & Helen

Angelina   Roy   Joanna

Helen divorces Dunn. She marries George Gifford, who adopts the three children. They take his last name. Megan's parents die. She is adopted by her Uncle Roy.

Angelina   Roy   Joanna
(m. Robert May)   (m. Cliff Parma)

Megan   Megan   Jake

Chapter One—The Psychology of Jake

Catastrophe. There was no other word for my life right now. I was hot. Sticky. Covered with feathers, everywhere but my face, hands, and feet. I'd become a freak. A seasick freak who was about to puke in front of a girl. This wasn't the way I expected this trip to go. Deep inside, I'd always known we'd have to go to Komodo Island to get rid of the curse. I didn't know—couldn't even imagine—how far away it was and how long it would take to get there. I was so tired I couldn't think straight, but I still had to focus on the positive. People were relying on me.

A cool washcloth came over my eyes. Someone was putting an ice pack on the back of my neck feathers. It wasn't the ice so much as the touch that comforted me. Kind and gentle. I opened my eyes. Beside me, a pink light glowed through a shell. Megan's necklace. I breathed a sigh of relief. That necklace gave me hope that this misery would soon be over. I'd be a normal kid again with skin instead of feathers. The hard cartilage shaft of each feather stuck into me like a knife, like a thousand knives sticking into my skin. Under these feathers I was still human. I wanted the feathers gone.

The metal rail that ran along the outer edge of the ship felt cold and damp on my hand. We were aboard a small freighter, a cargo ship that carried supplies to the islands. It was the last leg of a journey that had taken us three weeks. We'd left the last week in July, two weeks after Austin and I returned from camp. Now it was the middle of August, and we were almost there. We'd taken the back way to the back of beyond, to the place where a medicine woman had placed a curse on my grandfather and his buddy long ago when they were in the Navy. Why? Because Gramps's buddy had poked a Komodo dragon with a stick, and the Komodo had turned on him and bitten off his leg. The Komodo was about to eat the rest of the man when my grandfather shot it. What else was he supposed to do? Maybe if Gramps had known then what he knows now, he'd have stepped back and handed the dragon a fork. And maybe some ketchup. Then my brother Austin and I, our friend Megan, Gramps, and the others wouldn't be heading for an unknown island on an ancient cargo ship.

Food, clothes, tools, and medicine had to be brought to these tiny islands by ship because there were no stores where people could buy things. Some islands were so small there weren't even any houses. Or hotels or restaurants. People ate fish from the ocean, and the animals ate each other. Especially on the island we were headed for—Komodo Island. Komodo Island was the home of huge, ancient, scary dragons. Humans were on their list of prey.

Nausea washed over me again. I hung over the rail, my stomach turning inside out. My head was pounding.

"Luke, try a couple of sips of this. It might help." Megan handed me a bottle and poked the straw between my cracked lips.

I tried to sip. The soda tasted cold and sweet, and felt good on my tongue. But I doubted I could keep it down. Behind Megan I could see Austin and Jake, hovering. "Could you guys all leave?" I said. "I really don't need spectators." If there was anything worse than throwing up, it was throwing up in front of a crowd.

Jake took a huge bite of a hot dog and chewed noisily next to my ear with his mouth open. I groaned and faced the other way, keeping both hands on the rocking steel rail.

"Jake, I want you to see how that looks to others." Megan dug in her little purse and pulled out a mirror. She held it in front of her cousin's face as he chewed with his mouth open.

Jake smoothed his hair as he put his ugly face next to the mirror. "Good looking dude." He opened his mouth, picked something from behind his front teeth, and flicked it into the ocean.

Megan sighed and put the mirror away. "Are you afraid someone might like you if you acted like a normal human being?"

He jabbed his finger toward her face. "You're the one who isn't normal. Hanging around with bird-boy here and his sicko brother."

"You're talking about the kid that saved your life a month ago," said Megan. "If he hadn't dragged your carcass to the ocean you'd have ended in that pile of ashes."

The smug look on Jake's face hardened into a stony glare. He didn't like being reminded that I'd saved his life in the fire on Fish Island, where the campers had gone for an overnight. Megan didn't back away. She crossed her arms, threw her head back, and stared up into his face.

"Don't you have someplace to be, Jake?" Austin glanced at his wristwatch, ignoring the brown fur that hadn't gone away after his last morph into a grizzly bear. His problem wasn't as bad as mine, though. I was still almost entirely covered with eagle feathers. Even on hot days I had to wear long-sleeved shirts with hoodies that covered the feathers on my arms and head. Luckily, my face and hands were still human.

Jake hadn't moved a muscle. He and Megan were staring at each other, eye to eye, Megan glaring up and Jake squinting down at her.

"It's almost noon, Jake," added Austin. "Time to meet with your parole officer."

It happened so fast none of us saw it coming. Jake's hand moved in a blur, yanking the shell pendant from Megan's neck. Beads flew everywhere. Austin grabbed Jake's wrist but it was too late. I watched in horror as the shell pendant—still glowing pink—sailed in slow motion through the air and dropped into the churning seafoam about thirty feet below the rail that surrounded the deck. I tried to speak, but I couldn't make the words come out. All I could do was stare at the water, willing the necklace to fly back up into my hand. My brain refused to accept what Jake had just done. Without that necklace, I was doomed to a life with feathers. I'd never be able to finish school, or get a job, or even have a girlfriend. The necklace was my ticket back to Normal, and it had just flown into the sea. There was no way to get it back. There was no point in diving overboard. The ship was moving much faster than any of us could swim. The necklace was probably already at least a couple of football field-lengths behind us. My life was over.

Jake ran from the deck, laughing. Megan followed him to the stairwell but didn't go down. Her hand was at her throat—

a bright red cut showing where the necklace had scraped against her skin.

The next instant, a huge gray dolphin launched itself from the deck like a rocket. It soared about fifty feet over the water then splashed into the sea. Austin! My fast-thinking, brilliant brother had morphed into a new animal. He shot through the water like a torpedo, zooming beyond the end of the ship toward the place the necklace disappeared into the water. We ran to the stern and watched as the dolphin dove and vanished beneath the waves that rolled sideways in the wake of the ship.

I took a deep breath, shuddering. I couldn't believe all the things that had happened in the last two minutes. Only a minute ago Megan had given me a sip of soda. She and Jake had a stare-down lasting ten seconds at most. Jake had wrenched the shell pendant from Megan's neck and flung it into the ocean. And seconds later, Austin had morphed into dolphin form and propelled himself into the ocean. He was out there now, trying to find the shell pendant. In maybe forty-seven seconds, Jake Parma had managed to ruin my life. Again. Why had Gramps insisted on bringing him with us? Jake left a trail of disaster wherever he went.

I felt Megan's cold hand slip into mine. I glanced at her. Her face was red and sweaty, and she looked as if she was try-ing to swallow. The red line around her neck was starting to bleed. Jake had yanked that necklace so hard that the string dug into her neck before it broke. She should have turned death adder and bitten him for that.

Around us, the ocean glistened to the horizon in every direction. How could Austin find the shell pendant in these endless miles of water? Seconds went by. Then minutes. Austin didn't surface.

"Maybe we should call someone," I said. "Someone needs to ask the captain to stop the ship. Could you go get Mom and Gramps? They should know Austin's out there." I kept my eyes focused on the water, unwilling to move until my brother was safely back.

"Go yourself." Megan's hands gripped the rail. "I don't want to leave."

"Neither do I. He's my brother!" I frowned at her. Megan didn't look at me. She stood like a rock, staring in the direction the dolphin had gone. Drops of blood oozed from the cut on her neck. A purple bruise was forming along the line.

"One of us might have to go in after him," said Megan.

"The Komodo can swim really well, Megan. The turtle is too slow." Though I couldn't morph back into human, I could still go Komodo any time I wanted.

"The turtle has done just fine." Megan's tone was sharp. Where was this coming from? Maybe she didn't like taking directions from an eagle. Maybe she was forgetting that eagle was me. Plus turtle or not, Megan still wasn't much of a swimmer.

"You aren't experienced enough to swim in ocean waves," I said. "You could drown just trying to get away from the ship. Now please, just go get Gramps. Get somebody!"

Gramps emerged from the rear stairwell and walked toward us. A wave of relief washed over me, making my knees weak. I tightened my hold on the rail.

"What's going on?" asked Gramps.

I pointed toward the dolphin. Now I counted four dolphins out in the water, swimming in a circle.

"Austin's out there, Gramps." I explained what happened. As I was speaking, Gramps put his arm around Megan's shoulders. He was peering at the blood oozing from the cut on her neck.

"Jake caused that bruise," I said, "when he tore the shell pendant off her neck."

"I'll deal with him," said Gramps. "Is Austin okay?" Gramps knew I could sense the thoughts and feelings of animals. I'd had that ability since I first morphed into a Komodo dragon at the zoo the previous fall.

"I think so, but I'll check." I closed my eyes and tried to send Austin a message with my thoughts. *Austin, can you hear me? Are you okay?* I waited for an answer. Nothing came. I shook my head. Megan watched me, biting her lip.

In the distance I saw a dolphin leap out of the water and dive back in. An echo of laughter sounded in my mind. I felt happy, as though I could walk on air. I knew those weren't my feelings. They were Austin's feelings, or rather the Austin-dolphin's feelings. "He's okay," I reported. "He's playing with the other dolphins. I think he's moving toward us."

Gramps waved his arms in the air, then gestured for Austin to come in. The big dolphin stood on its tail, churning the water like the fifty horsepower motor I'd seen on a boat at camp last month. The Austin-dolphin flipped and sank sideways, but not before I caught a glimpse of something hanging from its mouth.

"He's got it!" I yelled. Tears filled my eyes, and I brushed them away with my sleeve. I was so miserable. Gramps patted my feathered shoulders.

"We'd have found a way to help you, Luke. With or without the necklace." Gramps turned me toward him and looked me straight in the eye. "You are not going to be an eagle much longer. So enjoy it while you have it."

"I stopped enjoying it when I was trying to haul Jake off Fish Island, Gramps."

My grandfather touched the long purple bruise on Megan's neck. "Jake did this?"

Megan sighed. "He broke the string when he pulled off the pendant. It really hurt."

"Luke, call your brother in, will you? I want him back on board before Megan and I go down to talk to Aunt Jo."

"There he is," cried Megan.

The dolphin leapt out of the water again, its slick gray body gleaming in the sunlight. A gray fin surfaced and swam near the big dolphin. Two more gray fins appeared, circling the water. I narrowed my eyes again, peering at them closely.

"Oh no!" cried Megan. "Sharks!"

"Not sharks. More dolphins." I pointed toward the triangular fins gliding just above the water. "See how the top of the fins curves backward a little?"

"I don't have eagle vision, Luke. I can't see things that are a half mile away." Megan bit her lip. "Which one is Austin?"

"Austin is the one with the necklace in its mouth," I reported with relief.

"Yay!" shouted Megan. "He did it!" She grabbed me and kissed my cheek. Usually that would have embarrassed me, but right then I was too excited and happy to care.

I smiled, still watching the water. I should have had more faith in Austin. If anyone could do the impossible, it would be my smart, super-talented brother. I kept my eyes focused on him to make sure he was okay.

The first two dolphins skimmed the water and dove

again. The other two glided along the surface until all four were swimming in a circle. They were playing, but I wished my brother would come back to the ship. With all that leaping and diving, he might lose the necklace. He might even swallow it. *Austin, bring it back!*

The biggest dolphin broke out of the circle and shot toward the ship. My brother must have sensed my thoughts. Ever since camp we'd been able to do that, especially when we were both in the form of animals.

Megan twisted her fingers as she looked at me. "I'm sorry, Luke. I should have gone for your grandfather when you asked me to."

I shrugged. "No worries. He came up on his own." I glanced at Gramps. He was standing several feet away from us, watching the dolphins with a pair of binoculars. I didn't think he could hear what we were saying.

Megan frowned. "There was nothing your grandfather could have done, Luke. I could have helped Austin."

I blew out a long breath. I wasn't in the mood for an argument. "He's my brother," I said again. "Getting the pink Komodo—finding it—is going to be hard, Megan. We can't be arguing if there's a crisis."

"So if there's a crisis I have to do what you say?" She sounded indignant. "What if I have a better idea?"

"That's okay. If your idea is better, I'll give in. But we might not always have time for a vote." I watched her face, trying to read her thoughts.

"It's like you always assume you're in charge." Megan crossed her arms and tilted her head to the side.

"I am in charge," I retorted. "I'm older and I know more. You and Austin are going to middle school next month. I'm going to high school. There's a world of difference." Megan stuck her nose in the air and turned away. Why was she being so difficult? She hadn't been like this at camp.

"There he is," called Gramps. Megan and I hurried to where Gramps was standing and hung over the side. The dolphin was swimming toward the ship, fast.

"Uh oh!" I bit my lip.

"What's wrong?" asked Megan.

"The Austin-dolphin is going to jump on board."

"Is that a problem?"

"Maybe. If he leaps up onto the deck, the other dolphins might follow him." One dolphin would probably attract the attention of the crew on the bridge. Four of them would have the whole crew down here. They might even have guns. I glanced around to see if there was anything the dolphins might destroy when they landed on the ship's deck. The nearest thing was the tall crane apparatus the crew used to load and unload heavy items. It looked pretty sturdy.

The lead dolphin swam toward the ship, gaining speed. It dove under the water, then shot upwards like a water spout, flying high into the air. It smacked heavily down onto the deck, showering us with water. Opening its mouth, the dolphin dropped the shell pendant in front of Megan. As she bent to pick it up, the dolphin rolled over twice, shrinking and melting away until nothing was left but the wet, grinning figure of my brother. It had all happened in just a few moments. It was unlikely anyone had seen it.

"That was great!" Austin sounded breathless.

Gramps nodded approvingly, then headed back downstairs now that he had seen Austin and the necklace were okay.

"That was some fast thinking, bro." I gave him a high five. "I'm glad none of them tried to follow you aboard." I glanced over the side. Three dolphins were still swimming alongside the ship. "Are they going to follow us?"

Austin waved to the dolphins. He was quiet for a few seconds. Then he said, "For some reason, they think we might need protection. So they're going to escort us for a while."

"Why would they think that? There's nothing strange about us. I have feathers all over my body. You just morphed from a kid into a dolphin and back again. We're on our way to an island where huge lizards occasionally eat people for lunch. I don't see anything odd or dangerous about this voyage, do you?" I perched carefully on the nearest deck chair. My stomach was turning upside down again. I might have to bolt for the rail.

Megan spread the length of the necklace between her hands. "Most of the beads are missing, but the pendant looks okay." She walked toward me, holding the shell in front of her. It began to glow, as though there was a pink light behind it. "Take it, Luke." She put the necklace in my hand. It began to blink on and off, casting light pink shadows on the deck. The blinking made me feel sick all over again, so I handed the necklace back to Megan.

"It's still working. That's amazing," said Megan. "Thank you, Austin. That was brilliant."

"It really was," I added. "I'm glad you were here."

"You'd have thought of something," said Austin. He smiled at me.

I shook my head. "I couldn't think of a thing. Neither the hippo nor the Komodo would have been any use. The eagle could have gotten out there in seconds, but I don't think it would've found the necklace in the water. They don't dive that deep." I glanced out at the miles of ocean around us. "How did you ever find it in all that water?"

"I had help." Austin gestured toward the side of the ship, where the other three dolphins still swam along next to us. "I heard the other dolphins singing about a quarter of a mile away. I sent a message out asking for any and all sea creatures to keep an eye out for it. The dolphins picked up the message first and telegraphed it to the other sea mammals. An orca was passing behind the ship and saw the necklace drop into the water. It sent a message giving the approximate location, and I took it from there. Luckily it hadn't sunk too deep. I found it easily."

"Let's not tell Jake that Austin got it back," said Megan. "He'll only steal it again."

"We shouldn't let him get away with this." Austin pushed his wet hair out of his eyes. "Jake has gone too far this time. Losing that necklace could have caused serious problems for all of us, but especially for you, Luke. We have to tell his mother."

"Fine with me. I don't care if they put him in the nearest lockup and throw away the key." I picked up the cold washcloth that Megan had put on my neck before Jake had grabbed the shell pendant and given her that ugly bruise.

"You need this more than I do, Megan. You should put some ice on that bruise."

Megan thanked me, taking the washcloth from my hand. The ice had already melted, but I was sure the cook would give her more.

We agreed to meet in the dining area in ten minutes. We also agreed that Gramps should be the one to tell Aunt Jo what

Jake had done. I was pretty sure he'd agree to speak for all of us. Megan and Austin went to their rooms to clean up. I stayed by the rail and watched the dolphins. They were swimming away from the ship now, diving and leaping off into the distance.

As I watched them, I thought about our coming discussion with Aunt Jo. What would we say? Jake would probably be at the table, listening. He'd probably argue with us, but it didn't matter. We had to stop this, now, or he'd keep doing things to sabotage our mission.

Jake seemed to enjoy making trouble for other people. A few weeks ago, when we were at camp together, he had pinched me, messed up my stuff, and made my life miserable, even though I'd never met him before. Then he shot off fireworks on Fish Island. Some of the hot material landed in the dry trees and bushes, starting a wildfire that burned down or charred every tree on the island. We'd barely escaped with our lives. Three campers were treated in the Emergency department of a nearby hospital for smoke inhalation injuries. One of them had a severe asthma attack and could have died. The camp director called the sheriff. Jake had been hauled off that night and locked in a special jail for kids who weren't seventeen yet. He totally deserved jail time, but somehow his father, a lawyer, got him off. Now Jake was on parole. That meant he had to check in with someone assigned by the court every week or so. If he didn't show up or got in any trouble again, he could go back to jail.

Gramps wanted Jake along on this trip, so he got special permission from the judge to take him with us. Gramps had made Jake promise to report to his mother at noon every day. We were supposed to tell Aunt Jo if he acted up. Jake was always doing stupid, aggravating things, but we never told on him. We had to remind Jake every day he was still on parole. One phone call from Gramps could get him thrown back in jail the minute we got back from our trip.

Footsteps interrupted my thoughts. Gramps and Austin were walking toward me. Austin had changed clothes but his hair was still wet. I wondered what Gramps would say to Aunt Jo about Jake tearing off Megan's necklace. How would Aunt Jo react?

Gramps clamped a hand on my shoulder. "Still sick?"

I nodded. "I'm really tired of it, too."

He held up something that looked like a small round bandage. "This should help. It's a seasickness patch. I'd have given it to you before, but you were never seasick on the other ship."

"The other ship was a huge, fourteen-deck ocean liner, Gramps. This is like a wobbly, oversized tugboat." I took a deep breath and retied the strings of my hoodie. I had to keep the hoodie firmly tied under my chin whenever I was out of my room. If I didn't, the wind would blow it off and the crew would see the helmet of eagle feathers that covered my head. That would be a disaster.

Traveling the last leg of the trip by freighter was actually a pretty good idea. This ship was small enough to dock in shallower water. It only needed about eight crew members to run it. They were busy working and ignored us. If I'd had two heads, no one would have noticed. The only problem I'd had since coming aboard the freighter was seasickness. I threw up about ten times a day. It was humiliating.

Gramps reached inside the hoodie and stuck the dime-sized patch behind my ear. I got up and walked back to the rail. Watching the horizon made me feel better. Gramps stayed next to me, and Austin was on my other side. He dug in his pocket and handed me a package of crackers. I opened one and bit into the dry, salty wafer.

"You go on to lunch, Gramps," I said. "Austin and I will be there in a few minutes." Gramps patted me on the back and headed for the stairway at the front of the ship.

This ship didn't have a restaurant. It had five levels, with Level Five being the lowest. On Level Two was a small kitchen, which the crew called "the galley." Next to this was a large table where we all sat together to eat. The bedrooms were on the next level down, Level Three. There were two stairways, one near the stern or back of the ship, and one near the bow. Austin and I went down the front stairway and stopped on the landing between Levels Two and Three to wait for Megan.

The dining area was right next to the galley kitchen. We were standing behind the door to the galley. Several members of our group were at the big dining table. They couldn't see us, but we could hear everything they were saying.

I opened the door a crack to see what was going on. Mom, Gramps, Roy Gifford, Aunt Jo, and Jake were seated at the table. Jake was talking to his mother. He looked upset.

"You left me with him." Jake's voice was strangled, as though he was choking on the words.

"I had no choice, Jake," said Aunt Jo. "The judge gave him total custody." Now Aunt Jo's voice sounded funny. "Because of what happened."

"Dad said you attacked him." Jake crossed his arms.

"Should we leave? Maybe you want to talk about this in private," said Mom. She rested her hand on Aunt Jo's arm.

"I can leave too," said Gramps.

Aunt Jo told everyone to stay. "You might as well hear this. I'm sure you're all wondering why Jake grew up without a mother when I'm alive and well." She took a deep breath. "That day, when I saw Cliff start to take his belt off, I couldn't stand it. I wasn't going to let him hit you, Jake. Before I knew it, fur started to grow all over me, and in about three seconds I was a wolf. I knocked your dad down, but I didn't hurt him. Just scratched his face a little."

"You turned into a wolf? In front of dad?" Jake's tone was angry.

"It happened so fast I couldn't believe it myself," explained Aunt Jo. "I'd never morphed before, so I really didn't know what was happening to me. I only knew that I had to protect you. My father used to beat us with a leather strap. I wasn't going to let your dad do that to you."

From where I was standing, I could see Jake's face. He was staring at the floor. His face was hard, as though he'd aged ten years.

Megan came up the stairs and stopped behind Austin. I put a finger to my lips, signaling them to be quiet.

"Your dad didn't tell the judge about my going wolf," Aunt Jo was saying. "The judge wouldn't have believed him. Your dad just said I attacked him and scratched his face. The judge gave him sole custody." Aunt Jo reached for Jake's arm, but he wrested it away from her.

"You'd have found a way if you wanted to!" cried Jake. "You never even came to see me." He jumped up, pushing his chair back.

"I couldn't." Aunt Jo sounded as if she was going to cry. "Your dad testified I was violent, so the judge suspended my visitation rights." Her voice faded into silence. "The truth is, I thought they were right to take you away. I didn't know how I turned into a wolf and I was terrified it might happen again. I certainly couldn't raise a child with that hanging over me."

When she looked up again, her face was pale. "I just didn't want you to be hurt. By either of us."

Jake snorted. "You think he never hurt me? You think you didn't? You're wrong." He stomped out of the dining area, shoving me out of the way as he came through the door. I fell forward, catching myself on the kitchen counter. Austin and Megan followed me into the room.

Mom frowned. "Were you three listening?"

"I'm sorry." I turned to face Aunt Jo. "But I'm glad I know. Now I understand a little more about why Jake bullied me at camp."

"Jake bullied you?" Mom and Aunt Jo said the words together, both looking shocked.

"It was nothing," I said quickly.

"It was plenty," said Austin. "His arms and sides were black and blue."

"Why didn't you tell us?" Mom's tone was strained. She sounded like that when she was trying not to get angry.

Austin explained. "He didn't report it or tell anyone. He knew he'd be sent to the nurse and she would find the feathers."

"It's Jake's fault Luke has all those feathers all over his head!" cried Megan. She explained how Jake started a forest fire during our camping trip to Fish Island. "When he realized what he'd done, he wouldn't move. It was like he was in shock or something. The fire was burning all around us, and everyone was getting in the boats. I couldn't just leave him there, so I stayed. I thought I could get him to swim for it. But when the fire got close, he just stood there like a statue. If Luke hadn't rescued us, both of us would've died on that island."

Aunt Jo gasped. Mom pressed her hand over Aunt Jo's.

"The island was three miles out in the lake," added Austin. "Luke had to turn eagle to get over there before the whole thing went up in flames. But when he tried to morph back..." Austin broke off and looked away.

Aunt Jo's eyes widened. "So you saved my son's life?"

"And mine," said Megan. "Then Jake goes and throws my shell necklace in the ocean. That necklace is the only thing that can help Luke get rid of those feathers. Jake doesn't even care that they're ruining Luke's life."

"Let's not forget about what he did to your neck," said Austin. He pointed to the angry purple line on Megan's neck. "Jake ripped the shell necklace off Megan's neck. Then he threw it into the ocean."

Aunt Jo looked from one of us to the other. Then she buried her face in her hands. She didn't make any sounds, but her shoulders were shaking.

"Don't cry, Jo," said Mom. She handed Aunt Jo a tissue. Aunt Jo dabbed her eyes with it.

"I don't know what to punish him for first. He should be grounded for the rest of his life." She took Megan's hand. "You poor baby. Look at this bruise." Megan's aunt touched the flaming red mark. "We'll put some ice on it." Then she turned to me, frowning. "Jake should never have thrown Megan's necklace in the ocean. But I don't understand what it has to do with your feathers."

I tried to explain it. "Once we've morphed into an animal, some of its traits remain even when we turn back into human form. For instance when I narrow my eyes, I can see things that are two miles away."

"An eagle trait," put in Austin. "When we went to camp a few weeks ago, Luke had a few little feathers under his arms. Every time he used an eagle trait at camp, the feathers spread. After he turned eagle to rescue Megan and Jake from the Fish Island fire, the feathers covered his head." I felt heat flush into my face. Everyone was staring at me.

Austin continued. "Luke can't have any kind of a life with those things." He pulled up his sleeve and showed the patch of brown fur on his arm. "Now it's happening to me. But Luke's problem is much more serious, and we have to get that curse removed to help him."

Aunt Jo looked up at me, her face sad. "I'm so sorry, Luke."

I shrugged. "It isn't your fault."

Aunt Jo stared into her coffee cup. "If I'd had more self-control, maybe I could have prevented myself from morphing. Then I could have divorced Cliff and gotten custody of Jake."

Gramps reached over and gripped Aunt Jo's shoulder. "I don't think any of us managed to control it the first time, because we didn't know what was happening. You have to stop it when you have the first tiny inkling that it's about to happen." He gave her hand a squeeze. "I'm sure telling Jake what happened was the right thing to do. Someday he'll understand."

"I hope so." Aunt Jo took a tissue from Mom and wiped her eyes.

Megan pulled what was left of the necklace out of her pocket. The shell looked the same, and the pink Komodo painted in its center was still there. But most of the beads were gone from the string, and the clasp was broken.

"Maybe I could try to fix it," said her aunt. "It's the least I can do. But I still don't understand how it will help Luke get rid of his feathers."

"Watch." Megan moved toward me. As she came nearer, the shell glowed pink. When I took it into my hands, the pink light began to blink on and off. "The shell glows whenever Luke is near," said Megan.

"Luke might be an eagle now," said Austin. "But it's glowing because Luke has also morphed into a Komodo dragon and retained some Komodo characteristics. We're pretty sure the shell will help us find a pink Komodo. We just aren't sure exactly how."

"You know the story of the curse, don't you, Jo?" asked Gramps.

"Roy told me a little about it," said Jo, with a nod to her brother. "Dad never told us anything. When I turned into a wolf, I didn't know what had happened to me. I didn't even tell my mom. I thought I was some kind of freak."

So Gramps told the story about how he and Dunn Nikowski had gone to Komodo Island when they were on leave from the Navy. They had been told to stay away from the Komodos, but Dunn poked one with a stick. It turned on him and bit off his leg. Gramps had to shoot it. Then he took Dunn to the island's first aid station. Dunn was unconscious and had lost a lot of blood, but they saved his life. After a few hours a medicine woman came in and waved a stick over them, saying some words Gramps didn't understand. The medicine woman's daughter was there too.

Dunn was very ill and had to stay on the island when their leave was over. Gramps went back to the ship. Before he left, the medicine woman's daughter reminded Gramps that the Komodo he'd shot was pink. This color was very rare, and the dragon was special to the islanders. Because of this, her mother, the medicine woman, had put a curse on Gramps and Dunn. This curse would affect their descendants as well. It would only be removed when they returned a rose-colored Komodo to the islanders. Each person would have the strength of three animals to help them find one. That was the part of the curse that turned us into animals.

"I didn't believe any of it," said Gramps. "Not until..." He gestured for me to continue the story.

"Austin and I turned into zoo animals on a school field trip." I completed his sentence. I didn't tell Jake's mother about everything that happened. I didn't tell her about the battle in the zoo parking lot.

"Megan and I were at the zoo that day," said Mr. Gifford. "Both of us turned into animals too. We were all pretty shocked." He leaned toward his sister, Aunt Jo. For the first time, I could see the family resemblance between them. "Dad left the family when we were kids," he added. "We never heard the story of what happened on Komodo Island."

I finished telling the story. "When we find a pink Komodo and return it to the people of Komodo Island, the curse will be removed from all of us."

Aunt Jo smiled. "Even me?"

"All of us," I repeated. "Gramps, Dunn Nikowski, and all their descendants were cursed—our whole complicated family. When we return the pink Komodo, the curse will be taken away."

"That's what the medicine woman said," echoed Gramps. "Her daughter explained everything to me the next day."

"Her daughter's name is Katerie," said Roy. "She was

Dunn's first wife."

"And she's my grandmother." Megan grinned. "I can't wait to meet her."

Chapter Two—The Passenger from China

The seasickness patch was working. I felt better, but I didn't think I could eat anything. I asked to be excused and went down the spiral staircase to Level Three, where the guests slept. There were four bedrooms and two bathrooms, divided by a large lounge where we could get together and talk or play games. We'd arranged for Mom, Aunt Jo, and Megan to have the bedrooms on one side of the lounge, and Gramps, Uncle Roy, Jake, Austin, and I to have the rooms on the other side. The lounge was empty. No music or talking came from any of the guest rooms. I found the room I shared with Austin and Jake and knocked on the door.

To my relief, Jake wasn't there. I sat on my bunk and tried to relax. Something was happening in my mind. I closed my eyes and tried to focus. A soft, fuzzy noise came over me. Someone—or something—was trying to make contact. The feeling gave me goosebumps. I'd had this sensation twice before, once at the zoo and once at camp. Each time the message had been from an animal asking for help. I was getting something like that now. There were no animals on the ship, were there? No, there couldn't be. Was a human trying to send me a message?

Lying on my bunk, I took deep, slow breaths. I was tired and could easily have fallen asleep. But something kept nagging at me. There were no words, just feelings that washed over me like warm water. Thirst made my tongue stick to the roof of my mouth. Hunger caused my stomach to growl. Deep homesickness that made me feel sad and hopeless. That didn't make sense. I wasn't homesick. Gramps, Mom, and Austin were on the ship with me. Something was wrong. I was getting feelings that belonged to someone—or something—else.

I sat up and found my flashlight and pocketknife. The men's bedrooms and bathroom were in the stern, so I was closest to the rear stairway.

I descended the metal stairs into darkness. Level Four had no portholes or windows because this part of the ship was under water. The air smelled like wood and seaweed and oil, all mixed together. From the stairs, I directed my flashlight down the long cargo aisle. Large crates and boxes were stacked one on top of the other, stored neatly on wide wooden platforms. These must be the goods, groceries, and other things that would be dropped off on the islands. Safety lights cast shadows into the aisle between the boxes. I could hear the rush of water against the heavy sides of the ship, only a few feet from me.

The feelings of hunger and thirst were so strong I was almost sick again. I stopped to take a deep breath, but the air was moist and smelled like animal poop. Thirst and hunger washed over me again. The feelings had to be coming from an animal. The animal was very weak. It was losing hope. I had to get to it. I would have to go lower—to Level Five. That was the very bottom of the ship.

It was so dark on the stairs I could hardly see. My heart began to pound and goosebumps rose on my arms, prickling my feathers. What was I going to find down there? Was it a large animal? Or a small one? Was it a wild animal that could be dangerous? Even tame animals could be dangerous when they were hungry and thirsty.

Step by step I descended, my small circle of light barely piercing the darkness. The sounds of rushing water echoed over the thrum of the engines. My foot hit something solid and I stepped out onto what must have been the deck of the lowest level. Beneath this level would be nothing but the curved bottom of the ship. Ahead of me was the engine room and the machinery that ran the ship. The heat was thick and fluffy around me, blasting from the hot machines. Arms outstretched, I flattened myself against the wall farthest from the clanging collection of heavy metal, worried that a sudden tilt of the ship might throw me onto something hot.

My pulse throbbed in my ears. With every step it grew harder to breathe. The air was damp and heavy, and smelled like wet animal fur and dog poop. I hadn't received any more cries for help. Perhaps I'd imagined the whole thing. Or maybe the caller had become too weak to answer.

"Where are you?" I called. My voice was hoarse from fear. I wanted to turn and run back up the stairway until I came to light and fresh air. But I couldn't. Something had called for help. Though I hadn't heard any words, I knew what it meant. An animal was in trouble. It might even be dying. I had to find it.

In front of me was a half wall that separated the engine room from the storage part of Level Five. As I walked carefully around the wall into the next section, my light caught on something metal. Moving the beam of my flashlight, I made out the shapes of three long tanks sitting end to end. Each tank was bigger than a van. There were gauges on top of the tanks. I crept slowly past them, directing the circle of light in front of me. A shuffling sound came from the other side of the tanks. I jerked to a stop. Something was moving. I took a deep breath to calm my thudding heart and peered around the end of the last tank. If I had kept going forward, I would have walked down an aisle that ran all the way to the front of the ship, almost the length of a football field away.

Running my hand along the boxes, I made my way toward the shuffling sound. The beam of my flashlight fell on the wooden slats of a crate that was big enough to hold a cow. It was empty except for a bale of hay in one corner. A tiny squeal made me jump. Beyond the empty crate was another large, rectangular crate with a hinged door on one side. Something black, white, and furry lay on its side across the far end. A round white head with small black ears lifted slowly from the hay. A thin, sick-looking panda stared back at me, its eyes still bright amid black furry circles that sagged into sunken white cheeks.

"Were you calling me?" My voice sounded strange in the stillness. I aimed the light into the panda's crate. Hay covered one corner and a pile of poop filled another. I looked for food but didn't see anything. I knew that pandas eat bamboo shoots all day long. I saw no bamboo shoots in the cage. Did it have water? A metal pail was tipped on its side. Empty. There would be a water supply somewhere for the people on board. I just had to find it.

Something skittered across the floor. Dark. Whiskered.

Long, pointed tail. A rat! Yuk. I wasn't keen on rats. They were good swimmers and could move through tiny pipes. They were smart and could get into your house through the toilet. They could eat your favorite breakfast cereal, or scare your mother, or even bite.

I listened again, hoping the sound hadn't come from the rat. But the rat didn't look or act as if it was in any distress. Whatever I heard or felt must have come from this sad, skinny panda.

Did you call for help? I sent the message with my thoughts, then waited for the panda to answer.

As the panda gazed at me, a wave of hunger made my stomach growl. I began to feel sick again. My mouth was so dry I could hardly get my lips apart. I longed for water. The messages were as clear as if it had spoken. The panda was hungry and thirsty. Then a feeling of sadness overwhelmed me. This panda was far from home. It longed to be free. What was going to happen to it?

I wasn't sure whether those were my own thoughts or the panda's. I pushed my hand between the wooden slats and very gently touched a furry black paw. The panda pulled it away. Then it closed its eyes and covered them with its fists. Turning away, it curled into a corner. The panda had pulled away from me, mentally and physically. I'd gotten the message, though. The first thing it needed was water.

I opened the latch on one end of the crate, reached in, and grabbed the empty pail. Then I refastened the latch carefully. I didn't want the panda to get out and jump overboard and try to swim back to China. That was where it must have been captured. I knew something about how animals were transported, because I'd once asked a zookeeper about it.

Zoos were very careful about transporting animals. They had to be examined by a veterinarian before they traveled. Some zoos required a vet to be on board. The animals had to have papers and proper care. Someone had to go along to take care of them. This animal was alone and neglected. This wasn't a legal transfer—I was sure of it. If it wasn't legal, the crew wouldn't want me to know it was here. I'd have to be very, very careful.

"I'll figure out a way to help you," I said. But even as I said it, I wondered what I could do for this animal. I could fill his bucket with water and get it back down to him. That would take care of the panda's thirst. But it was hungry too. Pandas spend forty percent of their time eating bamboo shoots. Had the person who caught the panda brought any food for it? We were going to Komodo Island. The panda wouldn't want to get off there. How could I get it back to China? I needed help. Tonight I'd get Gramps, Megan, and Austin together for a meeting. We'd have to put our heads together to figure this out.

I carried the bucket up the spiral staircase to the cook's deck, where the kitchen and the dining area were located. Mom, Gramps, and Aunt Jo were still at the table, playing cards. A big pile of poker chips was stacked in front of Mom.

She smiled at me. "Hi, Luke. Want something to eat?"

"No thanks. I was just... uh... looking for some water."

The cook came out of the kitchen, wiping his hands on his apron. He was staring at the bucket in my hand. His expression was angry, as though I'd done something terrible. He pointed at the pail.

"Where are you going with that bucket, son?"

"Just thought I'd get some water."

The cook glanced toward the back of the ship. "You went down to Level Five, didn't you." It wasn't a question, so I didn't answer.

"You shouldn't be below decks, boy," said the cook. "Nothing down there but engines. Nothing, got it?" His steely gray eyes bore into me. The message was loud and clear. I was to keep my mouth shut.

He reached out a gnarled hand. "I'll take that bucket too. Keep your hands off things that don't belong to you."

I felt a steadying hand on my shoulder, and Gramps moved in front of me. "I'm sure Luke was just curious about the ship, Mr. Burnell. Do you have any more of that soup left? He hasn't had anything to eat today."

The cook went back to the kitchen and reappeared with a bowl of hot soup and a package of crackers. Then he brought me a glass of soda.

"Below decks is no place for a kid," the cook said again. This time he was looking at Gramps and his voice wasn't so harsh. "Nothing down there but engines. They get hot. Kids don't belong down there."

I opened my mouth to tell him I just wanted some water for the panda. Then I caught Gramps's eye. He shook his head, ever so slightly. The cook went back to the kitchen. A few minutes later we saw him go down the stairs with the bucket in his hand.

"Don't mind him," said my mother. "Try some of the soup, or at least some crackers."

"Were you carrying that pail around because you were afraid you were going to be sick?" asked Gramps.

"No. I'm not sick anymore." I opened a package of crackers and took a bite of one. After making sure none of the crew was around, I told Gramps what I'd seen on Level Five. "I found a huge panda down there."

"What's that about a panda?" asked Austin. He and Megan joined us at the table.

"It's in a crate in the bottom of the ship," I explained. "It's starving and thirsty. I was just trying to get the poor thing some water."

Gramps glanced around the table. "Is everyone accounted for? Where's Jake?"

"He's in his room," said Aunt Jo. "I just checked on him. Anyway, Jake wouldn't choose to morph into a panda. Too tame."

"Uncle Roy is taking a nap," said Megan. "And the rest of us are here. So the panda must be real."

"It's real," I said. "It came from China and it wants to go back."

"They're probably going to try to sell it to a zoo," said Gramps. "Illegally, of course. Or maybe to some person who collects exotic animals."

I shook my head. "They aren't going to be able to sell a dead panda. And this one looks thin and dehydrated. I'm not sure it will make it through the night."

"That's so sad," said Megan. "I'd like to see it."

Gramps looked up. "I don't think you should go down there tonight. The cook is going to be watching. He looked pretty angry."

"Gramps, I have to get down there somehow," I said. "If I don't get water to it, that panda is going to be dead by morning."

"Dead by morning!" It was the cook's voice, but the cook wasn't here. A black bird flew through the air and landed on a corner of the table. It was about ten inches long with a glossy black head and a yellow bill. The body was brownish, with white-tipped tail feathers. Tilting its head to one side, it said, "I can talk. Can you fly?" Everyone laughed.

"A myna bird," said Gramps. "It must belong to the cook."

"Give us a kiss," said the bird. It sounded exactly like the cook's voice.

"There's something else," I said in a low voice. "There's another crate down there too. Empty."

Gramps sighed. "I'll bet good money that crate won't be empty when it leaves Komodo Island."

Mom stood up and stretched her back. "How far do we still have to go, Dad?" she asked.

"We should be there by tomorrow morning," said Gramps. "We've been making good time."

"Where are we going to stay?" asked Austin. "I did an internet search before we left home. There's nothing on Komodo Island but a tiny village. There were hotels on some nearby islands but they looked kind of primitive."

"Just so the Komodos can't get in," said Aunt Jo.

"I guess we could rent a boat or have someone take us to one of the other islands to sleep," said Gramps.

"And eat," added Austin. "I've been hungry for two days now."

I winced. I didn't like hearing that my brother was hungry. It reminded me too much of our time in the zoo. I glanced at Austin and found him looking at me. We both remembered those three terrible days when we'd been trapped in the bodies of animals. Austin was a grizzly bear and I was a Komodo dragon. I couldn't eat the frozen rabbits and rats they gave me. Austin couldn't eat raw fish. So I sneaked out at night to find food for Austin. I stood on my hind legs and used my talons to undo the lock. A Komodo could probably open any door that wasn't locked. But I decided not to mention this to Aunt Jo.

"You look awful, Luke," said Megan. "Have you been able to eat anything?"

"This soup is perfectly good," said my mother. Austin made a face. Mom sighed. "I have protein bars in my duffle bag. Help yourself."

"May I have one also, Mrs. Brockway?" asked Megan.

"Sure. Austin, please get one for Megan."

"Make that three." I shoved myself away from the table.

The cook reappeared in the kitchen. He didn't have the bucket with him. I hoped he'd filled it with water and left it in the panda's crate. I'd have to sneak down there again as soon as I could and make sure.

Gramps waved to the cook. "Mr. Burnell, is this your bird?"

"Maggie," called Mr. Burnell. "Come over here. Time to eat." He opened the refrigerator and took out a bunch of grapes. The myna bird flew to his shoulder and perched there, holding on with its horn-colored claws. Mr. Burnell cut grapes in half and fed them to the myna, one at a time. Maggie went into her cage, and the cook stayed in the galley, cleaning up. He busied himself putting pots and pans away and didn't look up as we passed by. He was watching me, though. I'd felt his eyes on the back of my neck several times while I was trying to eat. He'd catch me in the blink of an eye if I put even one foot on that spiral staircase in the rear of the ship.

Mom, Aunt Jo, and Gramps were getting ready to play

cards again. Small bags of potato chips lay on the table next to each of them.

"Luke, we're going to our lounge," said Megan. "Come on down."

"Don't forget about Jake," said Mom, glancing up at me. "Make sure you invite him to whatever you're going to do."

I gave her a look as if to say, *Are you kidding? After what he just did?* I lingered to see if she would realize what she was asking of us, but I didn't say anything.

I had other reasons I didn't want to invite Jake. Austin, Megan, and I had things to talk about. Secret things, like how to catch a pink Komodo. I didn't want Jake to hear any of it. He couldn't be trusted. When he heard our plans, he'd go straight to our worst enemy and tell him. That enemy was his grandfather, Dunn Nikowski.

For several months Austin and I had thought Dunn was dead. We'd seen him die in an epic battle with Gramps in the zoo parking lot. But after Gramps heard the story about the fire on Fish Island, he gave us some shocking news. He said Dunn could have survived that last battle by morphing into something small and going down a crack in the pavement.

That meant Dunn could have morphed into something very small again and hidden somewhere on this ship. When he turned back into his human form, the first person he'd go to see would be his grandson, Jake Parma. Jake was a bully just like Dunn. They were two of a kind. If they were together on this ship, we were in big trouble. But I couldn't say any of this in front of Aunt Jo. Jake was her son, and Dunn was her father. Poor Aunt Jo. She was caught right in the middle.

Right now, Aunt Jo was dealing cards to Gramps and Mom. Mr. Gifford—Megan's Uncle Roy, Aunt Jo's brother—

joined the game. Gramps was arranging the cards in his hand. He glanced up at Aunt Jo and asked, "Where did you say Jake was?"

"In his cabin. I didn't like his attitude or his sassy mouth. I told him to stay there until I came to get him." She looked at her watch. "It's been almost two hours. Maybe I should let him come out now."

"If he'd stayed in jail, he'd be confined a lot longer than that," said Gramps.

Aunt Jo went to the kitchen and spoke with Mr. Burnell. He gave her a plate of sandwiches, a carton of milk, and some cookies. Taking the food, Aunt Jo went down the stairs to Level Three. I started to follow her. Then I heard a voice call out, "Man overboard! Man overboard!"

"Oh no!" cried Mom. She jumped up and pushed her chair away. "I hope that isn't one of the kids!"

"Wait a minute," said Gramps. "I think the myna bird said that."

Mom sat back down. She was breathing hard and had red spots on her cheeks. "That was scary!" said Mom. "It shouldn't say things like that."

"The bird has no idea what she's saying," explained Gramps. "She just repeats what people have taught her to say."

"Give us a kiss," said the bird. "Pretty bird." She fluttered from her cage and perched on my finger.

"Who do you belong to?" I asked, carefully touching the bird's wing.

The myna tilted its head to the side. It didn't speak, but as it stared at me, a thought bloomed in my mind. Maggie the myna was telling me she didn't belong to anyone.

Do you know the panda? I asked the question in my mind, sending the thought to the myna bird. *The panda.* I kept a picture of the black and white bear in my mind, hoping the bird would see it. *It's in the crate next to the engine room. Please see if it has food. It needs food and water or it will die.*

The myna blinked. It looked back toward the kitchen. The cook had gone into his room, which was behind the kitchen. With one powerful flap if its wings, the myna lifted into the air and darted away. It stayed low, flying just above the deck until it got to the back of the ship. A second later, it had disappeared.

Could it have understood what I wanted? Birds had small brains. Mynas, parrots, and a few other birds could talk, but most experts say they really don't understand anything. They repeat words they've been taught so they can be part of the human group, just as they are a part of the avian group in the wild.

I licked my lips. My throat was dry and my head was beginning to ache. Dehydration—that's what was wrong with me. I needed water. So did the panda. I was sensing the feelings of a creature three levels below, in the bottom of the ship.

Another minute passed. I went to the refrigerator and opened the door. There were cans of soda, bottles of water, and cans of beer. I reached for a soda.

"Keep your hands out of my refrigerator, boy," said a gruff voice.

Gramps placed his cards face down on the table and pushed himself up from his chair. He walked out to the little kitchen. I was still standing there with a can of soda in my hand. Mr. Burnell had his hand out, waiting for me to give back the soda. Gramps sighed.

"We've paid good money to take this ship to Komodo Island," said Gramps. He placed a hand on my shoulder. "Are you saying the kids can't help themselves to a soda? This boy hasn't eaten in days."

Mr. Burnell shifted from one foot to the other. "I'm responsible for everything in this galley. I have to give an accounting."

The myna bird flew up onto Mr. Burnell's shoulder. "Give an accounting. Give an accounting."

"Get back in your cage," said the cook.

"Dead in the morning," said the bird. "Give us a kiss."

I sucked in my cheeks to keep from laughing. The bird was really funny. It was hard to believe she didn't know what she was saying.

"Luke." Mom's voice interrupted my thoughts. "Austin is calling you. Can't you hear him?"

Gramps patted me on the back and told me to go. I left in a hurry with the soda clamped firmly in my hand.

Austin and Megan were waiting for me on the next level down, in the lounge between the guest bedrooms. We'd agreed to meet there to talk about how we were going to catch a pink Komodo when we got to the island. On the low round table between the chairs were the things we needed for a planning session: maps, paper, pencils, a red marker, three bags of potato chips, and a six-pack of soda.

"How'd you get those sodas?" I asked. "Mr. Burnell just yelled at me for taking one."

"I gave him a fiver," said Austin. He pulled a can from the soda pack and opened it.

"I should have known." I settled myself in a chair. It wasn't very comfortable. It was like the chairs they have in the waiting rooms of doctors' offices.

"So how are we going to catch this thing?" Austin opened a bag of chips and held it out to me. "I remember when the DART team at the zoo tried to capture you. That was scary. I was afraid they were going to shoot you." He set his soda can on the card table in front of us, just as the ship tilted very slightly to the right. The soda can slid a little, along with an empty popcorn bowl and a couple of magazines. My stomach lurched, but it wasn't from seasickness. The memories from our time at the zoo still gave me nightmares.

"So did I. They came after me with nets and guns." I munched a couple of chips and drank some soda. I was starting to feel hungry. "I wonder if they have any peanut butter in that kitchen." Then I remembered the cranky cook. "The cook wouldn't give me peanut butter anyway. He'd have to make an accounting."

"Make an accounting!" yelled the cook's voice. The myna bird flew down and landed on the table. It tilted its head and looked at Megan. "Give us a kiss. Give us a kiss," it said. Megan laughed. Then she stood up.

"I have peanut butter and crackers I brought from home. You guys keep working on the Komodo-catching plan and I'll go get them."

I opened my small notebook. "We could rope it," I said. Austin and I had taken a roping class at camp. We'd brought a couple of ropes along so we could practice while we were on the ship. "Any other ideas?"

"Maybe we could find a tranquilizer gun. Gramps says there's a ranger station on Komodo Island now. They might have one. Maybe we could borrow it."

"It's a great idea, but they probably won't loan a tranquilizer gun to a couple of kids. They'd ask why we wanted it."

Austin nodded. "True." He reached in his pocket and held up a small bottle of pills. "What about these?"

Pills! Kids had gotten sick or in trouble for using prescription pills. They could be dangerous. Now here was my brother, holding up a bottle of capsules. "What are those, Austin? And where did you get them?"

"Don't get excited," said Austin. "These are totally legal. I bought them at the drugstore. They're one of those cold medicines that also help you sleep. Maybe we could give the Komodo four or five of these and put it to sleep."

I thought about it. Trying to rope the Komodo could be dangerous, to us and to the Komodo. It could bite anyone that got near it, poisoning the person with its venom. While we were trying it get it onto a wagon or into a cage, it would be rearing and bucking and trying to get away. It would be flashing those jagged teeth around, just waiting to bite someone and paralyze them with venom. Or would maybe just go ahead and eat them for lunch.

Tranquilizing it would be a lot safer. But how many pills would it take? Maybe Gramps could help us figure that out. I wrote "*Tranquilize*" and "*Ask Gramps*" in my notebook.

Megan came back carrying a jar of peanut butter, a plastic knife, and a box of graham crackers. She passed the food around. For a few minutes we ate and stared at the map of Komodo Island.

"That's a lot of territory to cover," said Austin. "Do we have any clues about where this rosy reptile might be?"

"Maybe." Megan pulled a worn-looking paper from her pocket and opened it. "This is the letter my grandmother sent with the shell necklace." She passed the letter to Austin.

"What's this little symbol under her signature?" Austin frowned as he peered at the paper. "Isn't that the same symbol you put on those bracelets you gave us?"

Megan had made bracelets for the three of us while we were at camp this summer. When I first saw the little heart on mine, it worried me. I thought Megan had put it there because she liked me. I liked her too, but only as a friend. When I saw that all our bracelets had the same little heart, I felt better. I didn't want to hurt Megan's feelings, or Austin's either. Austin liked Megan. A lot. He never took that bracelet off because Megan had made it.

"There's a circle inside the heart under your grandma's signature," said Austin. He pointed to the heart on his bracelet. "There's a circle in this heart too."

"Megan, did your grandmother ever tell you what that symbol means?" I asked. "Did she mention it in the letter?"

"No, she didn't." Megan's shoulders slumped as she twisted her hands. "Grandma wrote the instructions for making the bracelets, and she sent me those little hearts to put on them. I'm hoping she's still alive so she can explain it to us when we get there."

Megan had told us a few things about her family. Her parents had died when she was a baby, and she had no brothers or sisters. Roy Gifford, who'd come on the trip with us, was Megan's uncle. He adopted Megan after her mother—his half-sister—died. Jo Parma, Jake's mother, was Roy's sister and Megan's aunt. Jake was Megan's cousin. So she was related to half the people in our group. Austin and I were related to the other half, Gramps and Mom.

Megan, Roy Gifford, Jo Parma, and Jake had one other relative who was probably on this ship—Dunn Nikowski. Megan knew Dunn was her grandfather, but she never talked about him, or even admitted that they were related. I didn't blame her. If Dunn was my relative, I wouldn't admit it either. Because of Dunn, we were all headed to Komodo Island to deal with a curse that a medicine woman had put on him and Gramps fifty years ago. That curse was the reason I was covered with feathers.

Being covered with feathers is really awful. I couldn't take them off the way I took off my clothes. When I took a shower, I came out with wet feathers. It was hard to get them dry. I tried using Mom's hair dryer, but it took too long. Sometimes I was so tired I just went to bed wet. I couldn't wait to be free of them. First, though, we had to catch a pink Komodo dragon and return it to the people of Komodo Island. That task wasn't going to be easy.

I handed Megan the bottle of tranquilizer pills and told her about Austin's idea. Megan unscrewed the cap and sniffed it, frowning. "Yuk. These smell like dirt. How would we get the Komodo to swallow these?"

"Komodos will swallow anything," I said. "They'll eat a goat, horns and all."

"We could bury it in some meat," said Austin. "And put the meat on the end of a rope. When the Komodo gets sleepy, we'll rope it and tie it up."

"Then what?" Megan looked from one of us to the other.

I shrugged. "I guess we'll have to ask the medicine woman about that."

"If she's still alive," said Austin. He finished his bag of chips. Wadding up the bag, he tossed it into a nearby trash can. "She'd be pretty old by now, wouldn't she?"

"Probably near ninety. Lots of people live longer than

that," said Megan.

"I'll bet your grandma is still alive, Megan." I smiled at her. Megan's grandmother was the medicine woman's daughter, Katerie. She'd seen the medicine woman put the curse on Gramps and Dunn Nikowski all those years ago. Katerie had actually married Dunn and had a daughter with him—Angelina. But then Dunn had insisted she return to the United States with him. She didn't want to leave the island, so they divorced. Angelina was Megan's mother, who died when Megan was just a baby.

"It can't be any old Komodo dragon," I explained. "To undo the curse, we have to return another pink one. Maybe your grandmother will tell us how to find one."

"Wait, if the pink Komodo is already on Komodo Island, why do we have to catch it?" asked Austin, looking puzzled. "How can we return it to the people when it already lives there?"

I shrugged. I had the same questions.

Megan studied the map. Taking a pencil, she drew a circle around some tiny islands as she spoke. "Here's Komodo. Here's Rinca and Flores. I've read there are Komodos on those islands as well."

The myna bird flew away. A few minutes later she came back, landed on the table, and stared at me with beady black eyes. I stared back. Into my head came a picture of slender green sticks with white rings and leafy sprigs. Bamboo shoots! Had that message come from the bird? Focusing on Maggie's black eyes, I waited. Again I received a picture. This time it was of a white bag, the size of a big trash bag, stuffed full of something green and pointy. It was in a room with other bags and boxes. They didn't look like the boxes I'd seen on Levels

Four and Five, stacked one on top of the other. The myna was showing me a small room filled with large containers of food and this big bag of green stuff. Even if those were bamboo shoots, I didn't know how to find them. Maybe Maggie hadn't sent me a picture after all. I'd been thinking about how to find food for the panda for the last two hours. Maybe it was just my imagination.

Keeping my voice soft, I spoke to the myna. "Thanks for your help. Now you should go back to the kitchen and rest." The bird tilted her head and blinked. Then she flew toward the front stairs that led to Level Two and disappeared. I hoped she had gone into her cage. That myna had a loud voice, and I didn't want her coming along when I went down to Level Five. I wanted to go alone. Three of us would make too much noise, and somebody might catch us.

I got up, stretching. "I'm going to go lie down for a while." I tried to sound casual so Megan and Austin wouldn't be suspicious.

"Me too," said Austin. He stood up.

"Me too," said Megan. Both of them followed close behind me.

I stopped in my tracks. Austin nearly bumped into me. "Where are you going, Austin?"

"Same place you're going. To check on the panda."

"Me too," said Megan, peeking out from behind him.

Sighing, I turned to face them. "Okay. But we have to be really, really quiet. Megan, I want to warn you about something so you won't scream. There's a rat down there."

"Please." She rolled her eyes. "When we were at camp, I stopped a wild boar in its tracks so it wouldn't ram you guys. Like a plain old rat is going to scare me."

Then I remembered something I had read. Pandas ate bamboo shoots, but if they had nothing else to eat they would catch and eat rodents. Rats were rodents. I knew where there was a rat. And where there was one, there were usually more.

Chapter Three—Once a Rat, Always a Rat

We tiptoed single file down the winding metal stairs in the stern of the ship.

"What's all this stuff?" whispered Megan, as we passed Level Four. She gestured toward the goods stacked on both sides of the aisle that extended from one end of the ship to the other.

"Stuff they drop off at the islands, I guess," I answered.

"Man, it's hot down here," said Austin. Beads of moisture bloomed on his face.

I put my finger to my lips to give them the "Be quiet" signal and led then further down the metal stairs to Level Five. The noise grew to a roar. Because of my Komodo traits, I could still smell things that were far away. I could smell people, too. Megan had a sweet, soapy smell. Austin smelled like dad's aftershave tinged with odor of bear. On this level the smells of human sweat and panda poop blended with the scents of heat and oil. Then I heard voices. Austin tapped my arm. He'd heard them too.

Giving Austin and Megan a signal to wait, I eased past

the engine and stood behind the wall that separated the machinery and the animal crates. Someone was there, squatting next to the empty cage that stood in front of the panda's crate. The form had shoulders like a male, or maybe an older boy. There were only three boys on board. Me, the one behind me, and Jake. I ignored the skip of my heart and tried to calm myself. What was Jake doing down here? His body was turned away from me, his head bent toward something on the floor. A gravelly voice pierced the darkness.

"You'll do what I say, or you'll regret it. No animal is going to make a fool out of me."

Shivers tickled my spine and all my senses came alert. That wasn't Jake talking. I recognized the voice. The speaker was someone older and meaner; someone who still haunted my nightmares. Dunn Nikowski! Gramps was right. Dunn was still alive. Where was he? I'd heard his voice clearly, but I couldn't see him.

"What do you want me to do, Grandpa?" Jake stayed huddled near the floor.

"You're no help to me locked up in your room." Dunn spoke sharply, just above a whisper. "When I tell you what time to meet me, you be on time, understand?"

Jake nodded. He stood up, his shape unfolding into the muscled thug who'd bullied me at camp. If he turned around, he'd only be about five yards away from us. I froze, panicked. How could the three of us get away before he saw us?

He didn't turn around. Shoulders hunched, he stood looking at the floor. I looked too. Just to one side of Jake's shoe, I could see the dark form of a rodent. Its body was about seven inches long, not counting the long pointed tail. The head had a pencil-sharp nose and whiskers that wiggled when it talked. It was a rat, probably the same one I'd seen earlier. It was the perfect form for Dunn Nikowski. I drew back before it could spot me. I hoped the Dunn-rat wouldn't distinguish our smells from all the other odors on Level Five.

"This is what I want you to do." Dunn lowered his voice so I could barely hear what he was saying. "They want to catch the pink Komodo. We'll beat them to it. I know a private zoo that pays good money for the right stock. A pink one is worth thousands."

Behind me, someone drew in a sharp breath. I think it was Megan. She'd clapped her hand over her mouth, and her face was pale in the dim light.

"The crate has a Jakarta stamp on it," said Jake.

"Not Jakarta. That zoo already has one. Besides, they'd never take one that wasn't approved and certified and all that."

"I don't know, Grandpa." Jake's voice sounded anxious. "How will we get it there alive?"

Dunn's raspy voice crackled through the air. "I don't care if it makes it alive. I just don't want Kenwood and his grandsons to get it. And that nosy granddaughter of mine."

Megan gasped again. I turned around and gave her the "shush" sign.

"But what about the curse?" asked Jake. "If the pink Komodo dies, we won't be able to get rid of it."

"I don't want to get rid of it," croaked Dunn. "Right now we have powers that no one else has. We can grow into large animals that can take control of anyone, anytime. If anyone gets in our way, we just wipe them out. We need that power, boy. Power is the only thing that matters. No one else has power like this."

"Except the Brockways," said Jake. "And all your descendants."

I kept my head down, listening. My heart was pounding so loud I was afraid Jake could hear it.

"Who told you that? Who told you about my descendants?"

"Mom," said Jake. "Your daughter. Remember her?"

"You want your mouth slapped?" Dunn practically screamed at him. But since he was just a small rat, his voice didn't go very far. "Just keep sassing and you'll get it."

"Sorry," murmured Jake. I felt sorry for him. Both his father and grandfather treated him badly. But right now his grandfather was in the form of a rat, so there wasn't much he could do to Jake. Why was Jake so afraid of him?

"Go up the other stairway, the one in the bow," rasped Dunn. "I don't want those Brockway kids to find you here."

"I'm not scared of them," said Jake.

"I don't want them to know I'm alive!" Dunn's voice was angry now. "I don't want them to know what we're going to do. If they interfere with our plan, it will spoil everything. You'll go to jail, and I'll end up dead. Do what you're told and stay away from them."

Jake left, disappearing down the aisle between the boxes as he headed toward the front of the ship. A small skittering noise followed him. I stepped out of my hiding place in time to see the rat's tail disappear under a box.

Megan and Austin were right behind me. I lowered my voice to the barest whisper. "Did you hear?" Megan nodded. Her eyes were wide and her hands were trembling.

Austin dabbed at his sweaty face with his sleeve. "I can't believe it," he whispered.

I signaled to Austin and Megan to follow me. "Act natural," I whispered. Then I spoke in my normal tone of voice. "Here we are. Be careful, guys. These engines could be hot." I tried to keep my voice normal, but my heart was still pounding. Dunn was alive and on this ship. He was headed to Komodo Island too. He wanted to catch the pink Komodo to sell it! He didn't want to undo the curse! I could have these feathers for the rest of my life!

"I can't believe they've got an animal down here," said Austin. He and Megan eased past the chugging motors and around the wall to stand next to me. Jake had disappeared. But what about Dunn? He was probably still hiding between the boxes, listening to whatever we said. I didn't know what to do. I was so upset I could hardly think, but I had to warn my brother and Megan about Dunn.

"He's morphed into a rat," I mouthed. I pointed toward the bottom of the long wooden boxes stacked four high on the right side of the aisle.

"He's so cute," Megan said out loud as we stood before the panda. "Why does he have his paws over his eyes?" She reached in and touched the panda's arm. "Poor baby. You must be hungry."

The panda pushed itself into a sitting position. Megan put her hand through the wooden slats of the crate again, but this time she didn't touch him. As I watched in amazement, the panda placed its paw on her hand.

"It must be male," muttered Austin. "It would be eating out of her hand if we had any food for it." He glanced at Megan. "Are you going to make it a bracelet?"

"Maybe," said Megan. "He's so adorable. He'd look cute in one."

"He's not a stuffed animal. He needs food and water." I unlatched the end of the crate and got the pail. It was empty again.

"I'll go." Austin took the bucket from my hand. "There might be a water spigot in the engine room." He took the pail and disappeared around the wall.

"What's this mark on his crate?" asked Megan. She pointed to a dark blue circle around the initials JK. I hadn't noticed it before. Jake had mentioned it though, so he must have been in here. He must have seen the panda.

"Maybe that's where it's headed," I said. "A destination stamp. JK could mean Jakarta. There's a zoo there."

"There's nothing in this crate," said Megan. "I wonder why?"

I waited, watching her examine the empty crate next to the panda's crate. Megan was a smart girl. She'd figure it out.

"Oh no," she murmured. Glancing toward the place where the rat had disappeared, she lowered her voice. "Look."

When I saw the mark on the top of the empty crate, I was stunned into silence. I'd seen that symbol three times now. I saw it first on the little hearts attached to the bracelets Megan made for us at camp. Today I had seen it on the letter her grandmother wrote to her. Now here it was again, stamped on this big, empty crate. A circle within a heart. What did it mean? Whoever marked this crate knew about that symbol. My stomach clenched. I tried to take a deep breath, but my chest felt tight.

I put my finger to my lips to remind Megan that the Dunn-rat was probably listening. Then I spoke out loud. "Let's see if we can find anything for this panda to eat." I didn't tell her the myna bird had shown me a vision of bamboo shoots in a plastic bag. I didn't want Dunn or Jake to know about my visions, either.

Austin came through the engine room door, carrying the pail. "Sorry to take so long. The closest water was in our shower." I opened the crate for him and he placed the pail carefully in the corner. The panda flopped down on all four paws and stumbled to the bucket to drink. His fur hung loosely from his arms and stomach. He was weak and dehydrated. We had to find him some food, fast.

"Where would they keep bamboo shoots?" asked Megan.

"They're plants," said Austin. "So they probably wouldn't be in these boxes. Is there a cold storage unit somewhere?"

"They have meat and vegetables for meals while they're out to sea. So they must have a cold room." Dunn was probably still listening to us. "Let's go back up," I said. "Maybe we'll think of something."

As we neared Level Three, I recognized Gramps' voice. We stepped off the spiral staircase and walked through the hall that separated two bedrooms. Gramps and Mr. Gifford shared a room. The door was open, and Mr. Gifford sat at the desk, writing something in a notebook. Gramps was sitting on his bed. He looked up and waved as we passed by. On the other side was the room Austin and I shared with Jake. It had two sets of bunk beds covered with striped blankets. Austin and I were in one set, and Jake had the bottom bunk of the other. He was there now, lying fully dressed on his bunk. His arms were crossed and his face was red, as if he had a fever. When he saw us, he turned on his side and faced the wall.

"I'm going to my room," said Megan. "Call me when you go to dinner." Megan headed in the direction of the bedrooms where she and Mom and Aunt Jo slept, which were on the other side of the lounge.

Austin pulled his duffle bag out of the closet and un-zipped it. "I have some candy bars." He felt around in the bag, then started taking the clothes out and piling them on the bed. When he'd removed everything, Austin turned the bag upside down and shook it. Nothing fell out but a gum wrapper. "I had candy bars." He walked to Jake's bed and poked him in the back. "Where's my candy, Parma? I had a package of Snickers bars in here. Six candy bars. I hadn't even opened the package. Where are they?"

"Oh dear!" Jake put a hand over his mouth and raised his eyebrows. He talked in a high squeaky voice like a little kid's. "Did you lose your candy?"

Austin grabbed Jake's arms. In three seconds Jake was on the floor and Austin was lifting his mattress up to look under it. Austin was still as strong as a grizzly bear.

Jake rolled over and kicked Austin's legs out from under him. Austin fell backwards, whacking the back of his head against the corner of the desk so hard it started bleeding.

"Stop it!" I yelled. "Can't you see he's hurt?"

Austin pushed himself up and raised his hands in the air. He was trying to show Jake he wasn't going to fight back. Jake went after him anyway, pummeling Austin with his fists. Aus-tin tried to block the punches but Jake kept hitting him. Fling-ing myself on top of Jake, I yanked him off my brother and pushed him onto the floor. Jake swung at me. I ducked, then returned the punch, bloodying his nose.

"Knock it off! Now!" Mr. Gifford, also the Physical Educa-tion coach at our school, hauled me off Jake. Gramps was holding Austin back. Jake took another swing at Austin. I went for him again, breaking out of Mr. Gifford's hold. Gramps stepped between us.

"You guys cool off, right now!" he yelled. "What started this?"

We all pointed at each other.

"Your precious grandson threw me on the floor!" yelled Jake. "Just because I had taken his stupid candy bars!"

"Is that true, Austin?" asked Gramps.

Austin nodded. "I didn't hurt him. Then he came at me twice and smashed my head into the corner of the desk." Austin touched the back of his head. When he brought his hand away, it was covered with blood. "Then he hit me in the face. I still didn't hit him back. He kept hitting me, harder and harder." Austin was breathing hard, and his face was red. Bruises were starting to blossom on his jaw and under his eye. The back of his head was still oozing blood.

"Austin wouldn't fight back because of his karate skill," I told the men. "He could have hurt Jake if he'd wanted to. Jake had already hit him four times when I stopped him." I turned away. I wasn't going to apologize to Jake. Gramps could do whatever he wanted to me.

"I'm moving in here," said Gramps. "Jake, take your stuff and go across the hall with your uncle." Gramps went into the bathroom and got a cold wet washcloth for Austin's head. Then he went across the hall and got his duffel bag.

Jake picked up his bag, grabbed a shirt from the corner of his bed, and left the room, giving us the finger behind his back on the way out.

When Gramps came back, he took a closer look at Austin's head. "There's a gash here, Austin. I think we'd better have your Aunt Jo look at it." Aunt Jo was a nurse and had worked in the ER. Gramps went up to Level Two to get her.

"That was pretty slick, the way you rolled him from his bed onto the floor. I hope you don't get more fur because of that move," I whispered, after Gramps left the room.

Austin just shook his head and pulled up his shirt sleeves. Soft brown fur extended from his wrists up both arms. He pushed the sleeves down again. "I don't care. Pretty soon we'll be losing these animal traits."

I hoped he was right.

Austin sat down on his bunk. Touching the back of his head, he winced. "It's really sore. There's a bump under the cut." The washcloth on his head was already covered with blood. I knew scalp wounds bled a lot, because I'd had a couple myself. Austin had hit that desk corner pretty hard. I hoped he didn't have a concussion.

Aunt Jo and Mom both came down with Gramps. Mom had our first aid kit and a bowl of ice. Aunt Jo brought a small bag that contained a blood pressure cuff, a stethoscope, and a small flashlight, as well as some other supplies. She had Austin sit up in the desk chair so she could see his injury better. She pushed his hair away, dabbing at the wound with a clean washcloth. "This could use a couple of stitches, but I doubt there are any doctors around. I'll have to put a couple of butterflies on it. I can't do that unless I get some of this hair out of the way."

"You're going to cut my hair?" Austin pulled away and stared at Aunt Jo.

"We aren't near any medical facilities, Austin. We can't take any chances with an open wound. I'll just shave off as much as I have to so a couple of butterflies and a small dressing will stick."

She went to work and soon had Austin's head patched

up. She checked his pupils and his blood pressure, then had him lie down with an ice pack on the back of his head. Mom brought him a soda.

"Let us know if you feel nauseated or anything," said Aunt Jo. "I'll be checking in with you every couple of hours."

"This sucks," groaned Austin. "There's blood all over my new shirt."

"I can get that out," said Mom. "Hand it over and put on a dry one." Taking the blood-spattered shirt with her, she followed Aunt Jo out of our room.

Neither of us slept well that night. Aunt Jo came in three times to check on Austin. When she woke him up, he was groggy but seemed okay. When morning came, I was glad. I felt better, and so did Austin. Breakfast wasn't quite ready, so we sat at the table in the Level Three lounge and had a cup of coffee.

A loud squawk made me jump. The myna bird flew from the direction of the front stairs and landed on my shoulder. I reached up, holding a finger out in front of the myna's feet. It stepped delicately onto my finger and for a moment we were face to face. I blinked. As the myna bird gazed into my eyes, the strangest picture came into my mind. The cook and the captain were talking together in a small room. I could see gallons of milk and cartons of butter and eggs stacked on shelves behind them. Packages of bacon, hot dogs, and other meats were piled on another. That kind of food had to be stored where it was cold so it wouldn't spoil. The place looked like a walk-in refrigerator. It must be the "cold storage" room.

I stared at the bird's beady black eyes, and she stared into mine. I watched the cook open a large plastic bag and show the captain long, green stems with white rings, topped with frilly leaves. Bamboo shoots! So they did have food for the panda. Why hadn't they fed it?

"Luke? Do you want a snack bar or something?" Mom's voice broke into my thoughts. The myna flapped its wings and flew away.

I looked at my watch. It was only seven o'clock. Breakfast wouldn't be served until eight. My stomach growled. "I don't know, Mom. The cook threw a fit when I took a soda out of the refrigerator at lunchtime yesterday."

Gramps clamped a hand on my shoulder. "I'll go with him, Laura. That cook can be a little cranky."

Gramps and I went up one flight to Level Two, where we ate our meals. As we walked up the stairway together, I told Gramps that we hadn't been able to find food for the panda. "I think it's in the cold storage room, Gramps. Isn't that where they'd put bamboo shoots to keep them fresh?"

"I don't know anything about bamboo shoots," said Gramps. "Why don't we just ask the cook where they are?"

"No way! He'll be mad because we went down there again. Besides, I think there's something illegal going on with that panda."

Gramps put a finger to his lips. Two men were talking, somewhere quite near. To reach the dining area and the kitchen, we had to pass through a hallway. Following the sound of the voices, we stopped next to a door marked "Perishables." "Perishables" were things like meat and milk— things that could spoil if left out of the refrigerator. This had to be the cold storage room! We leaned against the wall with our ears next to the door.

"If anybody sees that animal, we could be reported." It was a man's voice, one I hadn't heard before. "The animal welfare inspectors, the environmental groups, and everybody else will be after us. I could lose my master's license. Why I let you talk me into this I'll never know."

Gramps made a talking signal with his fingers and mouthed the word "Captain Morrison." We stayed still. Only the door separated the cook and the captain from me and Gramps. It made me nervous. If they opened that door, they'd see us. Gramps patted my shoulder. I knew he was trying to tell me not to be afraid.

The cook spoke, his words cutting through the air. "It's those nosy kids. I didn't plan on kids being on this ship. If they'd stay where they're supposed to stay, they'd never have found the panda. Now they're filling its water bucket and trying to find food for it to eat."

"What's wrong with that?" asked the captain. "Any moron knows an animal needs food. If we go to all this trouble and end up with dead animals, we make no money." The captain sounded angry. I was glad. The cook needed somebody in charge to tell him he had to take care of the panda.

"We don't have too much food for him," said the cook. "Just this one bag full. I didn't realize they ate so much."

"That's your problem, Mr. Burnell. I've got things to do," said the captain. Footsteps drew nearer to the door, then stopped. "What's this other animal you want to catch? We don't have a lot of time in port. We'll drop off supplies to the rangers and a couple of places in that little village. A day at most."

"We'll hurry," said the cook. "One of the guests on board used to live on Komodo. He says he knows how to do it. His grandson will help us. We'll catch the animal and get back on board right away."

"Is this another big animal?"

"Yep. And it will bring twice the price of the panda," said the cook.

"You'll have to take the crate down on the freight elevator, like we did with the panda. Don't forget to bring enough food for it."

"There will be enough food." The cook laughed. "Anybody that makes trouble…"

Gramps pulled me away, so I didn't hear the rest. But goosebumps broke out on my arms and shivers ran down my back. Mr. Burnell was going to catch a rare pink Komodo to put in that crate. Dunn was the passenger who was going to help him. No reputable zoo was going to buy an animal that was caught illegally. There were people who collected animals for their private collections. I figured the cook was going to try to sell the panda and the pink Komodo to someone like that.

We ducked into the room across the hall and waited while one set of footsteps went up the stairs. That would be Captain Morrison, going to the main deck and the bridge. Where was Mr. Burnell? A door opened and closed again. I peeked out and saw the cook walking toward the stairs. He was carrying a big white plastic bag. Green leaves stuck out the top. He headed down the stairs, and I gave Gramps a thumbs-up. We waited until the cook was out of sight, then hurried to the kitchen. Gramps opened the refrigerator door and moved things around, trying to find snacks. He tossed me an apple and a cheese stick and took an apple for himself. We went through the door next to the kitchen and climbed the stairs to the main deck. A gust of cool wind greeted us. I pushed the hood away from my head and let the cool breeze blow through my feathers. It felt so good.

The weather had changed. The sky was so gray you almost couldn't tell where the sky ended and the water began. Gramps walked to the high fenced rail that surrounded the bow of the ship. Resting his arms on the rail, he looked out over the water.

"You said something yesterday about a talking rat," said Gramps. "You'd better tell me what you heard."

I took a deep breath. It made me sick to even think about it, but Gramps had to know. "You were right, Gramps. Dunn Nikowski is still alive."

Chapter Four—Shipwreck

"Dunn doesn't want the curse to be removed, Gramps. He wants the power to grow big, the way you both did during the battle at the zoo, when you were a hippo and Dunn was a crocodile."

"That ability is not going to last forever," said Gramps. "Dunn was on that island for a year after I left. He married the medicine woman's daughter. The medicine woman must have given him something extra, something we don't have. Otherwise he'd be dead, and that huge crocodile body would have disappeared. Only his artificial leg would have been left. He must have morphed again into something tiny, right when I was biting the crocodile in half."

"We heard the cook say he's going to try to catch a Komodo dragon. He also said two guests are going to help him." I peeled the wrapper from my cheese stick. "Those guests must be Dunn and Jake. How do we stop them?"

"First we have to find the medicine woman—or her daughter—and see exactly what we have to do to lift the curse," said Gramps. "We have to be free of the animal traits that are left in any of us." He turned to look at me, resting his arm on the rail. "That's why I wanted all of Dunn's descendants along on this trip, as well as my own, Luke. I was the one who shot the Komodo. I have to correct that wrong."

"You only did it to save Dunn's life, Gramps."

A loud screech pierced the air. Toward the stern of the ship, a trapdoor about six feet square pushed upward from the deck. A giant gray-green snout emerged, then two football-sized eyes squashed under layers of heavy eyelids.

"Gramps!" I cried. "It's a crocodile—it must be Dunn! The crew will see him! What can we do?"

Gramps pulled a walkie-talkie from his pocket and spoke into it. "I need help up here. Get emergency supplies in your pockets before you come up."

The huge head turned, scanning the deck. The croc's mouth opened, showing jagged teeth the size of a ruler. Two clawed feet and a wide, scaly body pushed through the opening, dragging a tail as long as a truck. The immense crocodile waddled across the deck, its body moving like a broken train. As it moved, it grew bigger and bigger, until it was the length of a two-trailer semi. It covered over half the space on the deck! The clawed feet slipped on the smooth concrete, and the huge scaly body began to slide from one side of the ship to the other. The ship began to rock violently back and forth in the water.

"Dunn must be out of his mind," said Gramps, grabbing the starboard-side rail so he wouldn't fall. He raised his voice so I could hear him over the noise of the croc slamming into things on the deck.

A rat ran out onto the deck and climbed up the giant crane. It waved one of its front feet in the air.

"The croc isn't Dunn, Gramps—Dunn is the rat! I yelled. "The croc has to be Jake!" I clutched the rail to stay on my feet. The ship listed to one side, then rocked back the other way.

"This was a stupid thing to do," Gramps yelled back. "He's going to sink us!" He looped one arm around the rail and spoke into the two-way radio again. "Mayday! Mayday! Get to the main deck! Prepare the lifeboats!"

My heart was thudding in my chest. I could only see one lifeboat. There were eight of us passengers, the captain, and eight crew members. I didn't think the lifeboat would hold all seventeen of us.

The crocodile's bumpy snout snapped shut with the force of a giant mousetrap, catching some of the lines and equipment in its jagged teeth. It careened sideways and every-thing on the deck slid with it. It smashed against the crane, knocking it from its platform. The rat ran down the side of the crane and disappeared. The weight of the crocodile and the fallen crane caused the ship to tilt steeply to the left. The star-board side of the ship raised gently out of the water as the fence and rail on the port side was submerged. Crates, equip-ment, deck chairs, and parts from the crane slid past us, crashed through the fence under the rail, and splashed into the ocean. I almost went with them, but Gramps grabbed me just in time.

"Gramps," I yelled. "What should we do?"

Before the words were out of my mouth, the ship began to level out. A humungous dolphin flopped across the deck, rolling until it was the length of ten vans placed end to end. Austin had arrived just in time, supersizing himself as he morphed. Flapping his tail fins, the Austin-dolphin propelled himself to the middle of the ship and stretched out lengthwise across the bow to make the ship level again. The croc waddled toward the dolphin's belly, jaws gaping open. Austin couldn't keep the ship level and defend himself against the crocodile at the same time. I had to do something to help him, and fast!

"The hippo!" Gramps and I yelled the words together.

"Let me do it, Gramps. I can take him!" I hadn't gone hippo since the zoo, so it took a few seconds for me to remember how it felt. My feet grew pads, and I pounded the deck with four strong hooves attached to sturdy, short legs. My body lengthened and grew heavier and heavier. Focusing, I pictured myself ten times the size of an ordinary hippo. Ten times as long, ten times heavier. Ten times as many teeth in a mouth that could open as wide as a cave.

I heard the screech of ripping iron. We were on a cargo ship, but only an old, small one. Gramps was shaking his head. He cupped his hands around his mouth and shouted to me over the noise. "The deck can't hold this weight."

"I need this size to take the croc, Gramps!" I yelled back.

I waddled toward the crocodile. "Give it up, Jake," I cried. "You're outnumbered two to one."

"Not for long," cackled the croc. Rolling toward the left side of the deck, the croc ballooned up into the size of two train engines. As it grew, the right side of the ship raised slowly out of the water again and the port side went under. The dolphin started to grow, but he wasn't fast enough or big enough to level out the ship again. He rolled toward us, flapping his tail to move himself away as he tried to avoid smashing into Gramps. Leaping up into the air, he flipped over the rail and cleared the ship by about fifty feet.

The croc rolled toward Gramps too. I got between them, ready to catch it in my huge jaws. "Gramps!" I yelled. "Try to get out of the way."

Gramps scrambled hand over hand, dragging himself up into the bow of the ship just as the crocodile slid past him. The rail gave way under the croc's heavy weight, and the monstrous beast fell into the sea with a mighty splash. The ship was tilted too badly to recover. It was taking on water now. The more water it took on, the lower it would go. Then it would sink completely. We had to get everyone off, fast.

Getting off was going to be perilous. There were two dangers in the water. One was the crocodile. Unless Jake got control of himself, everything in the water was at risk from the Jake-croc's snapping jaws. The second danger was the ship itself. When it went under, its tremendous weight would suck everything and everyone down with it. In the form of a dolphin, Austin could move fast enough to get out of its way. But any humans who fell into the water would either be tasty tidbits for the giant croc or get dragged under with the ship. I had to get in there and defend my family from the monster crocodile. I could help them get far enough from the ship to be safe. We had only minutes before it went completely under the water. I had to act fast.

Closing my jaws, I stood straight on my four hippo hooves and slid forward into the water. One of the jagged edges of the broken rail caught in my skin as I went past, digging in hard enough to draw blood. I plopped heavily into the waves my huge hippo body sinking at least four stories down into the ocean. I paddled hard, my stubby legs churning the water like a giant automatic beater. Soon I was clear of the ship.

Two bulbous, tire-sized eyes and the barest tip of the croc's snout floated just above the waves. Its entire body was submerged, but I knew I was bigger than the crocodile. My body was wider than one of those huge semis that make the road shake when they pass you on the freeway. The crocodile was shrinking itself, probably so he could be faster in the water. I probably outweighed him, but that wouldn't matter if I couldn't get to him. Sinking deeper into the water, I opened my cavernous mouth and waited for the croc to swim over me. Just seconds later, the crocodile floated past. I shot upward until he was just above my wide open mouth. I snapped it shut. All I got was a mega-mouthful of water and a couple of little fish.

Where had the croc gone? Maybe Jake had gotten control of himself. Now I had to focus on saving my family. I paddled furiously back toward the badly listing, partially submerged ship.

Gramps was still on the deck, hanging from part of the rail that ran around the bow. The water was up to his knees.

"Grab this, Dad!" yelled a voice from somewhere over my head. Mom slid a life ring down the deck toward him. Gramps caught it and put his arm through.

"Get the others out," I called. "Hurry!"

The Austin-dolphin swam up next to me, and we floated side by side. "Sharks," said Austin. "Right behind us."

I turned in the water. There they were, four gray fins circling just a few feet from me. My tough hippo hide was still bleeding from the gash I'd gotten from the broken rail as I went over the side. The sharks must have smelled the blood.

"I'll lead them away," I called. I slid back into the water, leaning away from the jagged, torn metal railing. Hippos are good swimmers. It didn't take me long to paddle out a good half-mile from the ship. All four sharks followed me. Then I turned in the water and snapped my powerful jaws to threaten them. I could have eaten all four of them if I wanted to. I'd grown so large the sharks were just trout-sized fish to me. The sharks got the message and took off.

The ship lay tilted in the water, listing at a sharp angle. Megan was standing on the edge of the rail, getting ready to jump in. She was going to land too close to the ship. Austin had seen the danger too. He drew up close to catch her. She jumped and landed on the Austin-dolphin's wide, gray back. Austin swam out about a hundred yards, and Megan slid off into the water. She sank under the waves, and a few seconds later the huge Megan-turtle appeared on the surface. She paddled close to the ship, waiting for the rest of our families. Some of them might make it into the lifeboat, but I didn't think all of them would fit. It was a good thing Megan had morphed so she could give them a ride. Austin stayed near the ship too. Gramps and the others were still on board.

The crew was trying to launch the lifeboat. They yelled directions at each other, trying to work the mechanism that lifted it up and off the ship. Finally it swung out over the water and slowly began to descend. The myna bird flew in frantic patterns, following it.

"Man overboard!" she screeched. "Dead by morning!" This time I was sure Maggie knew what she was saying.

I stared up at the starboard side of the ship, watching concrete and gray metal emerging like the belly of a whale. Something was jamming at my brain. In my mind, I saw a terrified black and white animal holding onto the top slats of its crate. "The panda! I have to get him out," I cried. "He'll drown!"

The poor panda. Was it under water already? It was on

the port side of the ship, the side that was going under the water first. Bears could swim, but the panda was weak from not eating. Morphing back to human, I clambered up onto the tilted deck next to Gramps.

"Gramps," I rasped. "I have to help the panda. What can I do?"

"The others first," panted Gramps. "Your mom. You might have to morph again, Luke. I can't do it. I keep trying but nothing happens." He reached out and touched my arm. His hand trembled. Gramps was growing weaker. Where was that blasted lifeboat?

Mom, Aunt Jo, and Mr. Gifford hung from the opposite rail, now far above us. Their feet were slipping on the steeply slanted deck. The captain was trying to throw them each a life-ring. Aunt Jo had propped herself on one of the large projections that was used for rope. Mom was positioning her life-ring in front of her, as if she was going to sled down head first.

"No!" yelled Gramps. "Put it behind you! Sit on it!"

It was too late. Mom was already sliding on her stomach. Her body was slanted to one side, and she was headed for the jagged edge of the broken rail. I reached for her, but she whizzed past me, cracking her head on the bent rail and zooming out over the water. The dolphin churned through the water toward the ship and dove. I held my breath until the Austin-dolphin emerged with Mom holding onto his neck. Blood was streaming down her face. In the distance I saw a gray fin cruising just above the water. The fin wasn't curved slightly at the top. Another shark! I should have stayed hippo!

"Shark!" I yelled. Mom was clinging to the Austin-dolphin. They were still about fifty yards from the turtle. In an instant the shark swam between the turtle and the dolphin.

Could Austin outrun it with Mom holding onto him? Another fin appeared, gliding along the top of the water. Two sharks began to circle Austin and Mom. Then, as if answering a prayer, four dolphins leaped out of the water and dove again. Emerging upward, they surrounded the sharks, cutting them off from Austin and Mom. The big dolphin went straight for the giant turtle and waited while Mom climbed onto its shell.

The crew was trying to maneuver the lifeboat nearer to the ship. The captain yelled something, waving his arms for us to come. Aunt Jo and Mr. Gifford both had life-rings looped over one arm. They'd watched Mom hit that broken rail and must have known they could be injured too. But there was no choice. They had to let go. We shouted for them, waving our arms and telling them to stay low and cover their faces. Gramps and I were up to our hips in water now. If the ship went down with us still aboard, we wouldn't be able to fight the pull of the ship's weight in the water. We'd be sucked under with it. The ship was sliding sideways into the sea, minute by minute. We didn't have much time.

"Go, Luke!" yelled Gramps. "I'll be right behind you."

There was nothing to do but let go. I edged over a bit and flattened my body so I'd miss the sharp edges of the rail. Taking a deep breath, I let myself drop into the water. At first the feathers cushioned me, but as I went over the edge I felt the sting of saltwater. The concrete must have scraped some of them off. My hood had blown off, but no one seemed to be looking. I was so tired I could hardly move my feathered arms. The water splashed over my face, going up my nose and into my mouth. I was sinking!

Suddenly my body lifted up out of the water. Something rubbery was beneath me, propelling me forward. I grabbed my brother the dolphin around the neck and hung on. When we were about a hundred yards from the ship, he rolled slightly and dumped me into the water next to Megan's wide, smooth shell. I dragged myself onto it.

Mom reached over and grabbed my arm. "Are you okay, Luke? Your back is bleeding through the feathers."

"I'm okay. What about your head?" I reached up to wipe some of the blood from her face. She brushed it with her sleeve.

Aunt Jo and Mr. Gifford had finally gotten off the ship, followed by Gramps, the captain, and Mr. Burnell, the cook. The crew dragged each of them into the lifeboat as the dolphin swam around them.

I couldn't stop thinking about the panda. "Austin!" I yelled. "I've got to go back. I've got to try to get the panda out."

"No! You aren't going back there, Luke." Mom had grabbed my arm.

"I'll go Komodo. They're great swimmers. It's trapped down there, Mom! Drowning!"

Freeing myself from Mom's hand, I dove into the water. Focusing, I changed into Komodo form and swam back to the ship. I found the stairwell at the back of the ship and started down, changing back to human again. By the time I got to Level Five, the water was up to my chest. The engine area was just ahead.

I came to the wall that separated the engine from the crates. The doorway to the main storage area was open, but mostly under water. I ducked and swam through it, then came up for air on the other side. The panda's head was at the top of the crate, its mouth pressed between the slats. I dove under the water and downward to the bottom of the crate. It was hard to open because of the weight of the water pressing against it. I felt for the bottom of the end panel, pulling it upward and shoving myself up through the water at the same time. I took a couple of deep breaths. My heart was racing from lack of air and sheer terror.

A few seconds later, the panda's head emerged next to mine. I could see his feet paddling in the water. I moved up to the wall that separated the crates from the engine room. We'd both have to dive to go through the doorway. I sent the panda a mental picture of what I was going to do. Taking a deep breath, I dove under the water, grabbed the edge of the doorway, and shoved myself through it. Something furry scratched at my back. Our heads came up out of the water at the same time.

Now we had to get back up through that stairwell to Level One, the deck. I started out, pushing my way through the chest-deep water, barely feeling the edge of the stairs. The panda followed me, swimming on all fours. The metal pail from the panda's crate floated along in the water, along with hay and globs of panda poop. We kept moving, pushing our way through it. We passed Level Four. Then Level Three. Paper cups, books, and a popcorn bowl floated past us. I thought about my room. It was just down the hall, still out of the water because it was on the port side. The right side. But there wasn't time to try to retrieve anything. We had to get off this ship before it went under the waves.

The panda was breathing heavily now, squeaking a little with every breath. We kept moving. Level Two. A couple of chairs bobbed in the water. I shoved them away so they wouldn't hit the panda in the face. Only a few more feet to go and we'd be at the deck level. Then we could swim out and away from the ship.

Something gurgled behind me. I turned around. The panda had disappeared. Something black and white rolled behind me. I grabbed its fur and pulled until the panda's head was above water.

"Come on!" I yelled. "We're almost there!" I slung my arm over its shoulder and across its chest the way they'd taught us in Junior Life-Saving class. I kept walking, dragging the heavy, furry body behind me as I pushed against the water. Level One—the main deck—was just ahead. I could see the edge of the water and the sky beyond it. Then we stalled. I pulled at the panda's body, but I couldn't get him to move. It felt like he was stuck somewhere. Taking a deep breath, I dove under to have a look. The water was murky, and I had to shove trash out of the way. One furry foot was stuck behind the stairwell rail. I freed it and shoved myself upward. I was tired and out of breath. We only had a few more feet to go. The panda didn't seem to be able to move any further.

Suddenly something pulled the panda up higher, taking its weight away from me. Relieved, I swam along behind it. A gust of air blew over me. We were out of the stairwell and our heads were above water. I, the panda, and Jake were all breathing heavily.

"Thank you for getting him," said Jake. "I was afraid I'd killed him."

"Come on," I said. "Help me get him to the dolphin. Austin can take him to the turtle." I didn't think Captain Morrison would allow the panda in the lifeboat.

Jake and I towed the panda over the submerged ship rail to Austin. The panda was so weak I was afraid he'd fall off Austin's back. I sent it a mental picture, showing it how to lie face down on the dolphin's back and hang on. Jake swam to the other side of the dolphin. I pushed and Jake pulled, and soon the panda was on top of the Austin-dolphin's wide back. He held on as Austin swam carefully out to the turtle, about fifty yards away.

The dolphin moved slowly, and I wondered if the panda was too heavy for the Austin-dolphin to carry. When they bumped up against the turtle's huge shell, I sent a picture showing the panda how to climb on. It stretched its arms—now thin and sagging from lack of food and fluid—toward the turtle. But the panda was so weak Austin had to push from behind as Mom helped me pull it up onto Megan's huge shell. Austin crawled up behind it, human again. He fell back against the shell, looking pale and exhausted.

The lifeboat passed us, the crew staring in amazement at our strange group. I counted the people in the boat. The captain and eight or nine others—one with a black bird on its shoulder—plus Aunt Jo, Mr. Gifford, and Gramps. Only then did I realize one of our group was missing. Jake! He'd helped me get the panda out just a few minutes ago. Where was he?

Panicked, I scanned the water. There was no one swimming or yelling for help. Was Jake still on the ship?

"Megan," I cried. "I don't see Jake!" I stood up on her back and waved to the people in the lifeboat. "We don't have Jake!"

Then I spotted him. He was still on the ship, standing at the stairwell opening, which was now just a few feet above the water. Austin sat up and edged toward the water.

"No, Austin. I'll get him." Standing, I pulled the hoodie off my head. Holding my arms out to the side, I felt the wind beneath strong wings that lifted me into the air. My legs shortened and sprouted talons. As an eagle, it took me just a few seconds to reach Jake.

"Leave me," he said. "I've ruined everything. I made the ship sink. Everything is gone."

"I don't care, Jake. I'm not letting you drown." He didn't move. I had no choice.

Landing on his shoulders, I dug my talons into his skin and lifted him, just as I had on the island. Ignoring his screeches of pain, I dragged him out into the water. Megan moved slowly toward us. I towed him as close as I could, then let him fall into the ocean. He just floated there, making no effort to climb aboard the giant turtle.

"Get moving, Jake, or we'll all get sucked under when the ship goes down," I yelled. Jake stayed put, bobbing like a dead fish.

"Shark!" I shouted.

Jake yelped and started to swim toward the turtle. Mom and Austin hauled him up onto the turtle's back. I landed next to him.

"I'm really tired of saving your butt, Parma," I said. My voice sounded strange. I seemed to be making an eerie screeching noise. Mom and Jake stared at me, mouths open.

"Sit down, honey." Mom handed me my hoodie. "Put this on and try to change back to human. Focus as hard as you can."

"I should have gone," said Austin.

"You did your share. I'll be fine." Why were they so worried? They should be used to looking at these feathers by now.

Mom watched me, the lines in her forehead deepening. Jake's mouth still hung open, his eyes fixed on my face. Even the panda's eyes were wide as it stared in my direction.

"If you can't change back, Megan and I will stay offshore with you," said Austin. "We can bring you onshore when it's dark."

"Can't I just wear my hoodie to cover the feathers?" I asked.

"You can if you want." Austin sighed heavily. "But the hoodie won't cover that beak."

Chapter Five—Rescue

"Beak? Beak! Oh no!" I cried—or, I should say, squawked. Reaching up, I tried to feel my head and face. But I had no hands. Long wings stretched from my body where my arms used to be. My feet had become talons, just as they were when I took off for Fish Island. Only this time, I hadn't gone back to ten percent human.

"Don't panic, bro," said Austin. "We can undo this. I'm sure of it."

Megan stretched her long neck to look back at us. "The lifeboat is coming this way. Everyone stay calm."

The lifeboat slid up next to us. The crew stared, but no one asked why two boys, a woman, a panda, and an eagle were riding on the back of an enormous turtle. Gramps handed Mom a thermos and a plastic bag.

"Rations," said Gramps. "Do you have room for me over there? Jake, why don't you take my place in the lifeboat."

With a final horrified gape at me, Jake scrambled off the turtle's back and into the lifeboat as Gramps held it steady next to the turtle's back. Then Gramps stepped over, holding onto Austin until he was able to sit down. The lifeboat pulled away, heading toward the distant shape of a mountain. Megan began a slow, graceful swim in the same direction.

"I don't suppose there was room in that lifeboat for all of us," said Austin.

Gramps shook his head. "I don't think so. It's better if they go. It's going to take them three or four hours to get to the island. They'll send help back."

"Maybe a fishing boat will come," said Mom.

Gramps nodded. "Maybe."

Mom waved to Aunt Jo and Mr. Gifford, then turned to Gramps. "Are you okay, Dad?"

"Fine. I came over to bring some food and a little moral support," he answered.

"What kind of food?" asked Austin, peering into the bag Gramps had brought.

"Raisins, nuts, and snack bars. We'll have to make them last," said Gramps. "We don't know how long it will take us to get to the island." He poured water from the thermos and offered everyone a drink.

Austin broke the snack bars in half and gave pieces to Mom and the panda. He reached around and put one near the Megan-turtle's mouth. "Don't bite me," he said.

"Hold it steady," answered Megan. She took the piece of snack bar and gulped it down.

He held a piece of snack bar under my beak. "I don't need one, Austin. Thanks anyway." I stared at the water. I could probably catch fish and eat those. That's what eagles did. That would leave more food for the others.

"There it goes," said Gramps. "You got Jake off just in time."

We watched silently as the freighter slid sideways into the water and disappeared beneath the waves. How deep was the water there? Would it sink to the bottom? Perhaps divers would go down and find it. They'd find my backpack with the rope in it, the one we were supposed to use to rope that special dragon. I had other stuff in that backpack too. A clean hoodie. My clothes were in my suitcase under the bed. Under the water. I didn't need them anyway. Eagles didn't wear clothes. All I had now were the clothes I'd been wearing when I morphed, and whatever was in the pockets. I'd been wearing the bracelet Megan made for me at camp, so that would come back when I morphed back to human. If I ever did.

"Our stuff," I said sadly. "All gone. What did you lose, Austin?"

"Nothing but money," said Austin. He bit into his snack bar, explaining between bites. "I can always make more. Stocks are going up. I'll sell some."

Gramps and Mom smiled. It felt good to see them look happy for a few seconds. It made me feel like everything would be okay.

I scanned the waves, watching for fins. The sharks were gone, and so were the dolphins. Peering down into the water, I watched for fish. Something gray swam past the boat. I took off, skidding over the water, and grabbed it. It wriggled away. After three more tries I finally caught one. I bit into it. Yuk. It didn't taste as bad as raw rabbit, but I didn't like fish even when it was cooked. I'd have to get a lot hungrier before I ate it raw. I flew back to the turtle and landed, then handed the fish to the panda. He took a big bite and swallowed it, then stuffed the rest into his mouth. That was encouraging. He was a bear, after all, and he was starving. Maybe I could keep him fed by fishing.

"Can I get anyone else a fish?" I asked politely. Everyone shook their heads. "How about you, Megan? Turtles eat fish, I'll bet."

She craned her neck to look back at me. "You're probably right. I might have to. I'm getting tired."

"Stop for a while," said Gramps. "Just rest in the water."

Megan stopped swimming. For a few minutes we floated along quietly.

Austin sat down next to me. "After we've rested, maybe I could go dolphin again and tow us in. Do we have a rope?"

"Just what's on these life-rings." Mom held her life-ring up so we could see it.

"There's not enough rope there to tow a giant turtle," said Austin. "We lost our rope on that ship."

"We lost everything on that ship," said Gramps.

"I have my wet pack," said Mom. "When you called on the two-way radio and said Mayday, Roy and I got stuff together as fast as we could. I've got our passports, some money, and my credit cards. I think Jo has her first aid bag."

"That's a relief," said Gramps. "At least we can get home again when we're ready." He patted Mom's arm. "Do you have any bandages in there? That's quite a gash on your head."

Mom didn't have any bandages. Gramps fished in his pocket and brought out a soggy handkerchief. He dabbed the dried blood on Mom's forehead away.

"That stings, Dad," she said. "Just leave it. We'll get some first aid on the island."

"Gramps touched my wing. "We will fix this before we go back, Luke. I promise you that."

I nodded. I really wanted to believe him, but it was like

wanting to believe in Santa Clause when you're ten. You want him to be real, but deep inside you're afraid he isn't.

I stared off into the distance to the place where the ship had been. There was nothing there. The water was endless, covered with sun pennies sparkling to the horizon. In a couple of hours the sun would set, and we'd be out here in the dark. How would we know where we were going? How would Megan manage to carry us all that time?

Then the miracle happened. I saw it first, when it was still a couple of miles away. A boat was coming! It was a very large fishing boat, big enough to carry all of us.

"A boat!" I shouted in my eagle's shriek. "It's about two miles away!" Everyone started to cheer.

A few minutes later the low growl of a motor rose just above the sound of the waves. Gramps, Austin, and Mom stood up and waved their arms in the air.

"We can probably get them to take the panda on board," said Austin. "But they'll expect the turtle to take off."

"Morph now, Megan," said Gramps. "Everyone get ready to swim."

They were all in the water when the boat slowed and pulled up next to us. I flew low, staying nearby. The captain and three crew members held their arms down to us. Another man unrolled a rope ladder.

"Thank heavens you came along," said Mom, as one of the men helped her over the side. "We'd have drowned out here."

The captain frowned. "I thought you were standing on some kind of life raft." He spoke English with an Asian accent.

"It sprung a leak and sank," said Gramps. "You came along just in time."

The captain narrowed his eyes. "Will that panda bite?"

"No, it's very tame. It's a pet," said Gramps. "So is the eagle. It can't fly too well anymore. It injured a wing."

"Can you take us to Komodo Island?" asked Mom.

The captain shook his head. "Nothing there. No hotels. No place to get food or new clothes to put on. Nothing there but big bad lizards. You go somewhere else. Another island. You get food. Call someone and let them know you are alive."

"He has a point," said Austin. "Especially about the food."

"That's all right," Mom told the captain. "We really want to go to Komodo Island."

The captain nodded. "If that's where you want to go, I will take you there."

"The rest of our group is in the lifeboat," said Gramps. "We should meet up with them first and make sure everyone is okay."

The captain introduced himself. "Patel Miklos," he said, shaking hands with Gramps. "This is my boat." He gestured at the men, who were busy putting gear away so everyone could sit down on the long bench that ran along the both sides of the boat. Another man was at the wheel, looking at a map. Captain Miklos gave some orders, and soon we were on our way.

I stood on the bench next to Austin, staring out to sea. There was something bobbing in the waves about a mile away. It wasn't big enough to be a fishing boat. The lifeboat! Six men were rowing. I whispered to Austin, telling him what I'd seen. Captain Miklos stared in our direction. I squawked a little and let one wing hang lower than the other.

When the lifeboat was about one hundred yards away, Gramps stood up and waved. There was no sound of a motor. Something must have happened to the engine. Captain Miklos called out some orders, and the fishing boat slowed. The crew dropped the rope ladder over the side again.

"Only the passengers," yelled Captain Miklos. "Not a crew that left women and children alone on a raft while they take lifeboat. Now you stay in lifeboat."

"Austin," I whispered. "Look at the man in the stern."

"Yes." My brother was frowning. We knew Dunn Nikowski had been on the freighter, even though we hadn't seen him in human form. We'd recognized his voice when he was in the form of a rat and yelling at Jake. He was even scarier as a human. Both Austin and I remembered the sting of the cattle prod he'd used on us at the zoo.

Dunn sat hunched over, trying to blend in with the other crewmembers. But I could see that Gramps had recognized him too. Gramps was staring at him, his eyes narrowed and his lips forming a line so tight they almost disappeared.

Captain Miklos reached down to help Aunt Jo, Jake, and Mr. Gifford climb up the rope ladder and into his boat. Mom moved over so Aunt Jo could sit next to her. Jake sat on the floor, next to the panda.

When the fishing boat was underway again, I whispered to Gramps, "Why did you let Jake come with us?"

Gramps bent his head toward me. "He's Jo's son. She wouldn't want him left behind in the lifeboat. He's just a boy."

A boy who'd just managed to sink a ship and nearly drown everyone. But I didn't say that out loud. Jake had been willing to go down with the ship rather than face what he'd done. The same thing had happened on Fish Island. Jake had accidentally started a fire that could have killed some of the campers. He didn't want to leave the island then, either. I'd had to drag him off that burning island with my talons, just as

I'd carted him off the sinking ship.

The fishing boat revved the engines and we started out, quickly passing the lifeboat.

"We'll send someone back for you," yelled Gramps, waving at them.

In the distance, craggy gray mountains pointed toward the sky. "Komodo," said the captain, pointing.

"How long will it take us to get there?" asked Mom.

"Three, maybe four hours." He smiled at her. "You want a soda? I have soda. Americans like that, right?"

"Right," I muttered. The captain frowned. I squawked, trying to cover my mistake.

One of the crewmembers brought us bottles of water and coke. Austin took an extra water and asked if they had a pan he could use to give water to the eagle and the panda.

"Maybe he won't want to use up his water on the animals," whispered Mom. "We have money," she said in a louder voice. "We'll be glad to pay you for the drinks."

They found a metal dish and poured a bottle of water in it. The panda turned to it and lapped greedily. Bald eagles usually don't need to drink water because they get it in their food, which is mainly fish. But I wasn't really a bald eagle. Inside the feathers I was still a kid, and I was really thirsty. I bent my head to the dish and pecked as fast as I could, but the water was already gone. The panda licked the damp dish until it was dry. I squawked quietly to myself, but Megan heard me.

"We have to get Luke something to drink," she whispered to Austin.

Austin asked a crew member if he could have a cup for his soda. The sailor pointed to a metal cup that sat on the deck. Austin poured soda into the cup and Mom held it for me.

It would have been better in a tall glass with ice cubes, but even as she poured it down my throat past my hooked beak, I thought it was the most wonderful, thirst-quenching drink I'd ever tasted.

A few hours later, everyone began to yell and make happy sounds. I didn't have to squint. As we grew nearer to the shore, steep hills loomed up in front of us. There were trees on the hills and flowers on some of the trees. Everything looked golden in the evening light. A long stretch of sand lay between rocky hills that almost touched the water. A rectangular pier about one hundred yards long and fifty yards wide jutted out from the sand. We were almost there!

My heart began to pound. We'd come such a long way to get to this place, and now I was kind of scared about what we would find there. This was an enchanted place, the home of mystical beasts. We were about to land on Komodo Island!

Chapter Six—The Medicine Woman's Daughter

It was hard for me to stay still when I really wanted to soar into the air and see the island. But I was supposed to be a lame eagle, unable to do much more than hop around. Austin stood back, gesturing for me to perch next to the rope ladder. I hopped up and grabbed the side of the boat with my talons. My heart jumped! The sand was pink! Would this be where we would find a pink Komodo? I half expected to see one sunning itself there. Further in the sand was white beyond the pink, and behind this, gray beach grass blended into the lower part of the mountains.

The fishing boat chugged in next to the pier. Two of the crew jumped down and wrapped the mooring ropes around cleats on the pier so the big boat wouldn't float away. Everyone stood up, unfolding and stretching their legs. I was already standing. As an eagle, I couldn't sit or lie down. All I could do was perch for hours on my talons.

Gramps had a hard time getting up after sitting on the deck of the fishing boat for three hours. I wanted to help him, but I couldn't pull him up with my wings. I didn't want to dig my talons into his shoulders the way I'd done with Jake. I'd only moved Jake that way because it was an emergency and I didn't want him to drown.

Mom was going through the money in her wet pack and conferring with Gramps. They wanted to pay the boat's captain. He'd saved our lives and given us water and soda. The captain repeated that he would be glad to take us to Flores, where there were places to stay and buy food. I wanted to convince Mom and the others to go to Flores and rest overnight in a hotel, but caught myself before I said anything. The hardest thing about being an eagle wasn't the feathers or having to stand all the time. It was keeping my beak shut!

The captain suggested that Mom and Aunt Jo go buy food and clothes for everyone and come back tomorrow. Mom shook her head and said they weren't leaving us. Then Gramps had another idea.

"Do you know anyone who has a houseboat?" he asked.

The captain squinted, furrowing his brow. He didn't seem to understand the kind of boat Gramps was describing. I almost spoke up, but again stopped myself just in time. Our group already looked pretty weird. We didn't need to make it worse with a talking eagle.

"I don't think he knows what that is," murmured Austin.

Gramps asked the captain to follow him to the beach and he'd draw the kind of boat he wanted. The captain shrugged, but climbed over the side of the fishing boat. After he jumped down onto the pier, he shouted to one of the crew. The man unrolled a rope ladder that reached from the side of the boat to the ground. Austin climbed down and held the rope for Gramps. It was only about a five-foot drop, but Gramps was seventy-two years old. Mom was always warning him not to fall and break a hip. Once Gramps was down, Austin held the rope for Megan and Mom. I flew off, landing on the pier and waddling awkwardly to make them think I was injured. Mr. Gifford climbed down and held the rope for Aunt Jo. Everyone looked weary and ragged from our ordeal. People were gathering on the beach to watch as we got off the boat. Megan glanced around, her eyes eager. She seemed to be looking for someone.

The captain narrowed his eyes at the panda. It had curled up in a corner of the deck. One of the crewmen poked at it with a stick.

"Don't do that!" yelled Jake. He squatted down next to the panda and stroked its paw.

I yanked at Austin's pant leg with my beak. He bent toward me. "It's scared of all the people. And it doesn't know how to get off the boat," I whispered.

"Do you have anything we could use as a ramp?" asked Austin. "The panda is scared. It doesn't know how to climb down a ladder."

The captain said something to one of the crew. They brought a long slab of wood and placed it at a slant between the side of the boat and the pier. Two men held it at the top of the boat's side, so it wouldn't slip. Austin crawled up it and asked the captain for a rope. I flew back to the ship and perched on the side to watch. A crewmember pulled up the lid of the long cupboard we'd sat on during the voyage. Inside the cupboard were life vests, tools, and fishing equipment. Coils of rope were piled in a corner. Austin found a piece that was several yards long and held it up.

"Could I buy this from you?" he asked the captain. "And another one the same length, if you can spare it." We had figured out we needed about one hundred feet of rope. Austin and I had been practicing with lassos on every ship's deck since we left home, but neither of us could rope anything farther away than thirty or forty yards. The captain moved things around in the cupboard and found another length of rope. He coiled it and handed it to Austin.

Austin took a bill from the wet-pack around his waist and gave it to the captain. Then he handed another bill to a crewman in exchange for a six-pack of Snickers bars. When he'd tucked the candy away, Austin looped the rope around the panda's neck. He started to lead the panda down the ramp, but then hesitated. Smiling, he offered the lead rope to Jake. Jake's eyes widened. Straightening his shoulders, he took the end of the rope in his hand. He squatted down and talked to the panda.

"We're going down this ramp now. There's nothing to be afraid of. No one will hurt you. You'll stay right by me, okay?" Jake slowly led the panda down the ramp.

"You made his day," I whispered to Austin as we followed the panda.

"I doubt anyone has ever trusted him very much," said Austin.

"Can't imagine why." We laughed, but it felt good to see Jake look so proud. I was proud of my brother, too. Austin was always kind. Maybe I could learn to be that way.

On the beach, Gramps was trying to help Captain Miklos understand what kind of boat we needed. Gramps found a smooth patch of sand and picked up a stick. He drew a half circle, made it look roughly like a boat, and then drew a house on top of it. The captain laughed and patted Gramps on the back. He was nodding vigorously, pointing to himself.

"I have," he said. "I have this." He pointed to the house-boat. "You want to sleep in it, yes?"

"Yes," answered Mom. "And eat in it too." She made motions as though she was taking soup from an invisible bowl with a spoon.

"I understand, missus," said the captain. "I have pretty good English. I can get you some food. You have money?"

"Most of it went down with our ship," said Austin. "But I have a little left." He took two twenty-dollar bills from his pack and handed them to Mom.

"Thank you, Austin. I should have known you'd have money."

"Had money," said Austin. "It's almost gone."

Mom glanced at me. I was going to tell her I didn't have anything but my pocketknife and small flashlight, but caught myself again and closed my beak. I limped in a circle, dragging one wing as if I was trying to fly away and couldn't.

"You should kill that bird," said Captain Miklos. "It can't fly or catch fish. One of the Komodos will get it." He reached forward with two strong brown hands. "Here, I kill it for you. Wring its neck." Squawking, I dragged my wing and hopped like a jackrabbit away from him.

"Um, I don't think so," said Austin, reaching out to stop me. "I'm going to keep it as a pet. It's very tame." He petted my head, getting me in a headlock at the same time. "The panda is tame too, but we'd like to get it back to its home. Do you know anyone who is going to China?"

The captain frowned at Austin. He looked closely at the panda. "Sell to a zoo," he said.

"It was caught illegally," said Gramps. "No papers. No respectable zoo would buy it. So we want to find some good people who will return it to its home. Pandas are an endangered species. You understand that word?"

"What... you think I'm from Mars?" The captain pointed to the sky. "Of course I understand. Even in English." He appeared to be thinking. "I have idea. A way, maybe. I make a call."

He glanced at Mom and Aunt Jo, who stood there watching us, eyes wide. "You ladies sure you don't want to go to Flores? Many shops. You can buy things."

"Thank you," said Mom. "We want to stay here. Can you bring the houseboat to us tonight so we can sleep on it?"

He nodded. "We can do that, but it will take time. I must go home and get it, and then buy you some food." Mom gave the captain the money, and they shook hands. The captain got back in the fishing boat, and they pushed away from the pier. We waved to them as the boat moved slowly away.

Two men stepped forward and said they were rangers and in charge of the park. They wore khaki shirts, beige cargo pants, and black floppy hats with a Komodo National Park logo on the front. Both carried a long, sturdy stick split into a "Y" at the end. This was their only weapon.

One ranger asked why we had a panda and an eagle along. Gramps explained about the panda and said the eagle had been injured. It landed on the ship and Gramps was trying to heal it.

"They're friends," explained Austin. "The eagle can find its own food, but the panda is too weak. Stuff might start floating in from that shipwreck. Watch for a plastic trash bag filled with bamboo shoots."

The rangers spoke to each other for a minute, their voices low. They were speaking English. Then one of them turned to us and said, "Bamboo shoots grow here."

I almost shouted with joy but I covered the sound with a squawk. Austin and Megan stepped in front of me.

Austin said, "Could you tell us where? The panda is really hungry. We're afraid he's going to starve to death."

"I can take you there tomorrow," said the ranger. "It's about four or five miles up into the hills." He pointed to an area where the tree-dotted hills blended into a kind of forest.

"We have to find a way to get the panda back to China," said Austin. "We're pretty sure it was on that freighter illegally. Of course the captain and the crew will tell you something different if they ever make it to shore."

"Is there a place the eagle and the panda can sleep?" asked Gramps. "We don't want them to become Komodo food."

"We have an office and sleeping quarters near here," said the ranger. He gestured toward a small building in the distance. "There is a room we use for storage out back. It's almost empty. We could make a bed for the panda there. It doesn't look well."

The panda was sitting on the ground, slumped over as though it was exhausted.

"It's hungry and thirsty," said Austin. "Do you have some fresh water we could give it?"

The ranger nodded. "Let's get it over there, and I'll find a big pan for water. It looks so weak. I hope it can make it up the stairs. All our buildings are on stilts. I'm sure you can figure out why."

"The Komodos can climb pretty easily," said Megan. "I've seen them do it." Austin gave his head a tiny shake, rolling his eyes in Aunt Jo's direction. "I saw that in the zoo," Megan added quickly.

"We have doors that lock. Windows, too." He smiled at us. "What about the eagle? What does it need?"

"I'm not sure," said Austin. "It seems lame. It stays pretty close to us."

The ranger laughed. "Good decision."

More people had gathered around us on the sand. They were laughing and pointing to the panda. Probably they'd never seen one. The panda sat upright, watching the people. No one came close or tried to touch him. Everyone was respectful to both of us.

Suddenly the crowd became quiet. They stepped aside, making way for a woman who was walking toward us. She was about the same age as Gramps, or perhaps a little younger. Her face was kind and had very few wrinkles. She was dressed in a long cotton skirt and a loose white top, and wore sandals on her feet. The sun caught a few red strands in her gray hair. She stopped suddenly, putting her hand over her mouth as she stared at us. Megan gasped.

The woman stepped forward and so did Megan. They stood about ten feet apart for several seconds. Neither of them seemed able to speak. Tears filled the older woman's eyes. "Angelina," she whispered. "You look just like her. You must be Megan." She opened her arms and Megan flew into them.

"Grandma!" cried Megan.

"Yes! Yes!" said Katerie, the medicine woman's daughter. She hugged Megan, rocking from side to side. "I've read your letters over and over. I was afraid I'd never see you." The woman stepped back, still holding Megan's hands and gazing at her. "You're so beautiful! Just like your mother," she cried. They hugged again. Megan's shell necklace was glowing pink.

It always glowed pink whenever I was nearby, because I'd been a Komodo dragon. There were lots of Komodos around here, so it probably would be glowing all the time.

Where had the shell necklace gone while she was in turtle form? Probably the same place our clothes, wallets, watches, and anything else we had on went when any of us morphed—off into the universe of mysterious missing atoms. According to Gramps, everything was made of atoms, even the things we wore. When we morphed, our clothes, jewelry, and stuff in our pockets were absorbed into our new forms. Everything went back to its original shape when we became human again.

I bumped my wing against Austin. He was watching Megan and her grandmother, smiling. "They're happy," he said, glancing at me. He leaned against a tree, sighing contentedly. When Megan was happy, Austin was happy. If she wasn't happy, he wasn't either.

He couldn't read Megan's thoughts like I could when she was in animal form, though. Why did I have the ability to hear or sense what animals were communicating, when Austin didn't? I'd also been able to communicate with both of them through my thoughts when they were in human form. I wondered what the medicine woman's daughter was thinking. I stared at her forehead, focusing hard, but nothing came through. She glanced at me, and I quickly looked away. Could she feel me staring at her, even when I was in the form of an eagle?

Gramps stepped forward and spoke to the medicine woman's daughter. "You probably don't remember me," he said. "I was the sailor who came here with Dunn Nikowski all those years ago. My name is Raymond Kenwood."

It was funny to hear Gramps say his name. Mom called him "Dad" and we called him "Gramps." I was pretty sure the kids at the university called him "Professor Kenwood."

"This is my daughter, Laura Brockway, and Megan's aunt, Joann Parma." Gramps smiled.

"I am Katerie," she said. "I remember that you didn't want to leave, but you had to go back to your ship." Her eyes were still bright with tears. She took a handkerchief from her pocket and blotted her eyes. "I don't use Nikowski anymore since Dunn and I have not been married for many years."

"Dunn was with us on the ship that went down," said Gramps. "He's in the lifeboat with the crew. They should be here in a few hours." He placed his hand on Mr. Gifford's arm. "This is Roy Gifford, Dunn's son by his second wife." Mr. Gifford shook Katerie's hand.

Gramps introduced Austin, and Jake. I toddled along behind them, dragging my wing. Katerie turned to me and stood still, so I did too. She gazed at me intently for a few seconds. I sent her a mental message telling her I was really human under all these feathers. I wouldn't have had to, though. A jolt of recognition zipped between us like a buzz of energy. Katerie smiled. I tried to smile back, but my hard beak wouldn't curve upward.

"Does the eagle belong to you also, Raymond?" she asked, keeping her eyes on me.

Gramps nodded. "I'm afraid so." He gently touched my wing. "This is my grandson, Luke. My grandsons have suffered greatly because of the curse. That's why we've come from the other side of the world to see you and your mother."

Mom and Aunt Jo stood near us, watching. I looked up in time to see Mom wiping her eyes. It was the first time I'd seen her cry about my condition. It made me sad too. Everything in me ached to become human again. I longed to walk freely and run and swim with the other kids. I wanted to eat ice cream and pizza and spaghetti. I wanted to lie down in a bed and put my head on a pillow instead of perching upright all night with my head in some awkward position. But I knew it wasn't going to just happen. It would take something big. Something really hard. My life was already so hard right now that I didn't know if I could deal with any more problems. If only Katerie could help me right away.

Katerie smoothed the feathers on my head. "You must have been very brave."

"It's not only me." I said the words in a low voice, so the villagers wouldn't hear. "My brother, my friend Megan, my grandfather, and the others have also morphed. All of them have suffered too. Can you help us undo the curse?"

Everyone was listening now. Gramps had his arm around Mom. Mr. Gifford stood close to his sister, Aunt Jo. Austin reached for Megan's hand. She took it, and placed her other hand on my wing. Megan's shell necklace glowed with pink light. Katerie's eyes seemed thoughtful as she gazed at us. Then she caressed Megan's shoulder and gently touched the necklace.

"The necklace has no beads," said Katerie.

"It broke," said Megan. She did not look at Jake, who was standing behind Mr. Gifford and his mother. "The beads were lost, but the shell is the most important part, right?"

Katerie nodded. "Most important. For finding pink Komodo."

Someone behind me swallowed a sob. It could have been Mom or Aunt Jo. But it was a sob of relief, like the end of a crying spell. The medicine woman had placed the curse on Gramps and Dunn Nikowski all those years ago, but her daughter had just said she would help us. The air softened with relief.

Katerie turned to look at the panda, who was sitting under a tree, accepting food from the village children. "And the panda bear?"

"Real," said Gramps. "It was on our ship, and the boys managed to save it when the ship went down. We'd like to help it get back to China."

Katerie sighed. "So much suffering caused by evil and greed." Then she put one arm around Mom's shoulders and the other around Aunt Jo. "Come with me," she said. "You must be tired and hungry. Everyone in the village knows that your ship went down. Our supplies have gone down with it. But we are preparing a feast with what we have, and the fire will warm you if you are cold."

Mom said it was quite warm, and she was fine. It was probably ninety degrees, so we didn't need a fire. Aunt Jo shivered, but I didn't think it was because she was cold. She kept glancing around and biting her lip. Aunt Jo was very, very afraid here. I didn't blame her. She was probably the only one of us who had any sense.

A delicious smell wafted through the air. It smelled like pork. I hoped someone would toss me a piece.

"Wild pig," said Katerie.

I jerked my head around. Where was Jake? I hoped they weren't going to be serving him for dinner. Then I saw him, still standing with his mother and his uncle.

"The delicious smells always draw visitors from the hills," said Katerie. She pointed to the edge of the tree line, where two Komodo dragons crouched on thick, bowed legs. Their yellow forked tongues flicked out, tasting the air for prey. The islanders had built a barbecue area further down the beach, and the dragons knew dinner would be ready soon. They probably smelled the panda, too, and thought he was some kind of dessert. Some of the village men ran at the Komodo, waving big sticks with forked ends. Children yelled and threw rocks. The Komodos backed away, but they didn't go very far. I could see their tails, curled around some nearby bushes.

Katerie saw me looking at them. "We will give them food." She nodded in the direction of the scaly tails. "We aren't supposed to, because the rangers say it makes them lazy and they won't hunt. But we don't want them hunting our children. It's better if they aren't hungry, especially while you are here."

"You can give them my portion," said Aunt Jo. Her face was very pale as she twisted her hands together. She was staring at the Komodo dragons. I wished she hadn't heard us talking about them.

"Are you all right, Jo?" asked Gramps.

She shook her head. She wasn't "all right." Megan's aunt was terrified of Komodo dragons. She had good reason to be. They were dangerous animals that would prey on humans if they were hungry. Luckily, they only needed to eat about once a month.

"Sit here." Katerie took Aunt Jo's arm and led her to a smooth log near the fire pit where she couldn't see the Komodo. The villagers in the circle smiled pleasantly at us all and gestured their welcome. "I'll bring you some special tea, Mrs. Gifford," Katerie added. "You also, Mrs. Brockway."

"Call me Laura," said Mom. Her voice sounded steady again. She sat down on the log next to Aunt Jo.

"Don't worry, Jo. We'll watch the Komodo," said Gramps. "I won't let them eat you."

Aunt Jo narrowed her eyes, scanning the area around us. I'd already scoped the place out. The Komodos had backed far enough away that the humans around the barbeque area couldn't see them. I could see them, though. Two big ones were still hiding behind some scruffy bushes. It would take only a few seconds for them to scurry into the circle, grab one of us, and take off into the hills. I stayed alert, making sure I knew where they were at all times. I couldn't defend myself as an eagle. I'd have to fly somewhere out of their reach. If they were threatening anyone in our families, I'd have to go Komodo or hippo. I hoped I wouldn't have to do that in front of the villagers.

I whispered to Austin, "How big would a hippo have to be to take one of those Komodos?"

Austin shrugged. "I don't know. You're the animal expert." He nodded toward the women who were serving the food. "The villagers don't seem too worried about them. They just throw rocks or poke at them with sticks if they get too close."

"See that long branch there?" I flapped my right wing toward a slim branch with several leaves on the end. "If they start wandering over here, you could put one end in the fire to make a torch. You could wave it at the Komodos to keep them away."

"Or I could turn myself into a twenty-foot-tall grizzly," mumbled Austin. "That would keep them away too." He looked me up and down. "Aren't you tired of being a lame eagle? Why don't you go Komodo for a while? At least we could feed you a decent meal."

"I'm trying to keep an eye on the Komodos. I can do it better as an eagle."

Austin nodded. "Okay. I'll make sure you get some food."

We gathered around the fire. Everyone sat on logs or in a bamboo chair. I stood on the ground next to Austin. Katerie served us chunks of roasted pork on large, flat leaves. She placed a leaf on the ground in front of me and put a piece of roast pork on it.

"Eat," she said. "You will need your strength." Our eyes met, and she nodded. I was comforted, because she knew who I really was. She would help me get rid of the feathers and the beak and become a normal kid again. She would help all of us.

Chapter Seven—The Hole in the Whole

After we ate, Katerie gathered Megan, Austin, Gramps, and me together. "There is someone you must meet," she said. We followed her to a small hut on the outskirts of the village. Like the other huts, it was built on stilts. In front of the hut, a very old man sat in a bamboo chair. When he saw us, he smiled. He was missing several teeth.

Katerie introduced us to the man, saying a name I couldn't pronounce. She explained that he was the village Elder, and knew everything about all the people who had lived there during his lifetime. She said he might know where to look for the medicine woman.

We greeted him respectfully, each bowing our heads a little. Gramps put out his hand, and the elderly man shook it. He waved his hand, inviting us to sit down. There was a stool for Gramps to sit on. The rest of us sat on the ground next to the Elder's chair. Katerie explained what we wanted, then stood by to translate in case we didn't understand the Elder's words.

Gramps told him what happened that day when Dunn

Nikowski poked the Komodo dragon. The Elder knew the story well, because he'd been a young man when it happened.

The Elder poked a bony finger toward Gramps and said, "The shot you fired that day did not cause the curse. It was the other man's lack of respect for the animal. For nature. For that which was part of the Whole." When he said the word "Whole," he made a circle with his hands.

Gramps's eyes widened and he took in a sharp breath. "Wait!" He held up his hand as if to stop the Elder from speaking. "I don't understand. I was the one who killed the Komodo."

The Elder nodded. "You did what you had to do to save the other man's life."

Katerie clasped her hand on Gramps's shoulder. "He will explain further, Raymond. Then you will understand."

"The Komodo is sacred to us," continued the Elder. "For years we have lived together and no one was bitten. Then people began to visit the island to look at our dragons. Some came to camp here and study them. They wrote many papers by oil lamps at night. They were friendly and respectful to us. They bought our carvings and other things we made from bamboo. That gave us money for things we needed. When the freighter ship comes, it brings many things we must buy. Tools. Food. Clothing. Medicine." His eyes moved toward the ocean. "Your ship went down. Perhaps it was a bad ship. Perhaps it was cursed also."

"Dunn Nikowski was on the ship. That's why it was cursed," muttered Austin. I didn't think he meant the Elder to hear him.

The Elder turned his head toward Austin and nodded. "Yes. That may be true." He reached into his pocket and took out some white cigarette papers and a pouch of tobacco. He offered it to Gramps. Gramps thanked him but shook his head. Then the Elder offered it to Austin, who also politely refused. The Elder sprinkled tobacco into the paper, rolled it up, and twisted one end. He lit the end and a small flame flickered and died, leaving an orange glow on the end of the paper. The Elder drew on the aromatic cigarette and puffed.

He raised his eyes to Gramps. "You were there that day. You shot the Komodo." Gramps nodded, his face sad. "You saved that man's life," said the Elder. "The curse was not your fault. It was his." Gramps's shoulders jerked back and he seemed to be trying to swallow. The Elder went on.

"The dragon was sitting peacefully. The other man provoked the dragon by stabbing it. It was that man who put the hole in the Whole." As he said the word "hole" the Elder put his thumb and finger together to make the shape of a circle. When he said the words "the Whole," he formed a great ring with his arms, just as he had done before.

"So the hole made by Dunn's disrespect was like a wound to the earth, the great Whole," added Austin, making the large circle with his arms as the Elder had done.

"You are very wise for one so young." The Elder smiled at Austin. Then the Elder gently touched my wing. "You are very brave." I wished he'd said I was wise. But I was standing there covered with feathers and a wicked beak where my mouth should be. My brother was dry and comfortable and taking a Snickers bar out of his pocket. It was pretty clear which one of us was wise.

"Tell us about the wound in the earth," I said.

The Elder waved in the direction of the ocean. "You know about our coral reef?"

I nodded. "I've read that it's the best scuba diving spot in the world."

"The reef is part of the Whole, and it is wounded." The Elder pointed to a hut near the end of the village. A bright red chair with an attached canopy sat in front of the hut. Next to it was propped a silver bicycle with red and gold streamers hanging from the handlebars.

"The man who lives there is a fisherman," explained the Elder. "He has suddenly become very wealthy. He takes more fish than he needs from the ocean, far more than his family can eat." He waved his hand past several huts. "He takes more fish than the village can eat. But he does it in a way that damages the reef and turns it brown. He kills many species of fish with the blast of a bomb that contains dynamite or chemicals. This man gets rich, but he makes our village poorer by harming the reef. He makes a great wound in the Whole." Again he made the circle with his arms.

"Can't the rangers stop him?" asked Austin.

The Elder shook his head. "It seems a simple thing, but it isn't. Some of the men who come to buy his fish carry guns. The rangers do not carry guns. But let us talk now about why you are here."

He puffed on the cigarette and blew out rings of smoke, as if echoes of the Whole. "All of the trouble seemed to start after your friend poked the pink Komodo with a stick. It was disrespectful. That Komodo didn't threaten or hiss. There was no reason to poke her. She bit your friend in her own defense, and you were forced to shoot her." He nodded towards Gramps. "The medicine woman's curse was your punishment. She instructed the two of you to find another pink Komodo. You had to go back to your ship. Dunn was too ill for many weeks. After he was better, he did not try to find another pink Komodo. He laughed at medicine woman. Then he married her daughter." The Elder sighed.

"We want to undo the curse so we can become human again," I said. "To do this, the medicine woman said we must replace the pink Komodo that Gramps shot. We came here to find one and take it to the medicine woman. We don't know how to do that. Can you help us?"

Megan had stood quietly by all this time, watching. The shell on the string around her neck glowed pink. The Elder gestured to her. "You are the granddaughter of Katerie? She has been waiting for you a long time." He pointed to the shell with a shaking finger. "May I see this?" As Megan pulled the necklace over her head, the light caught on the little heart that dangled from the bracelet on her wrist. He looked at it closely, then nodded.

"You already have the secret," he said. "You have what you need to find the pink Komodo." He pointed to Austin's bracelet. "You have one also. That means you are part of find-ing it. "Then he looked at me. "You have a bracelet?"

I shrugged my eagle wings and shuffled awkwardly on my talons. "It will come back when I become human again," I answered. Then I had a terrible thought. What if all three bracelets worked together? Mine was off in the atmosphere somewhere, its atoms temporarily suspended. "Do we need all three bracelets to find the pink Komodo? I can't get mine until I return to human," I cried. "And I can't return to human with-out finding the pink Komodo."

The Elder reached out to touch my wing. "No, no. Be calm. I will help you. The Komodo you seek lives in a cave. She is very old and will not harm you. The three of you will go there together. You will be safe."

"Are you sure this is the Komodo we need?" asked Austin.

The old man nodded. "Roux hatched from one of the eggs laid by the Komodo your grandfather shot."

"Roux?"

"That is the name the medicine woman gave to the hatchling," said Katerie. She drew in the dirt with a stick. R-O-U-X. "There is an X on the end, but it is pronounced *Roo.* My mother gave her that name because La Roux means redhead or red-skinned in French."

"She is very old now," said the Elder. "Perhaps she is dying."

My heart jerked in my chest as terror washed over me. If the pink Komodo was dying, we had to hurry. If she died, I would be doomed to life with a beak.

"Where is she now?" I asked. The words came out in a croak.

The Elder pointed to the hills. "She waits there in the hills for you, in a place most humans don't go. It is dangerous there, because the Komodos are very wild. Here they wait for us to feed them, but in the hills they are not so lazy."

Behind me I heard Megan gasp. I turned to see if she was okay. Her face was pale, and her hand was across her mouth.

"You have what you need to protect yourselves," said the Elder. He was nodding at Megan. Did he mean Megan could protect us? Or was he talking about the shell pendant?

The Elder spoke again. "First you must find the medicine woman. She is very old and hasn't long to live. I have told you what you need to know. Go now. There is little time left."

He was growing breathless and looked tired. He'd just

said he'd told us what we needed to know, but I hadn't a clue what he meant. We'd learned that a pink Komodo named Roux lived in a cave, up in the hills somewhere. He'd also said both Roux and the medicine woman were very old, and probably dying. We had to find them, and fast.

Katerie went back to her hut, and Austin, Megan, and Gramps started to walk back toward the pier. Night had fallen, but we could see in the bright moonlight. I limped a bit, then flew in front of them and landed again. They quickly passed me, because as an eagle, I couldn't walk fast enough to keep up with them. I didn't want to just fly, because then I couldn't hear what they were saying about the Elder and our task. Finally Austin picked me up and carried me.

No one spoke for a few minutes. The air around us was hot and heavy with the weight of the task we had to accomplish. I didn't see how we could manage this alone. But the Elder seemed to think it was up to the three of us—Austin, Megan, and me—to break the curse.

We stopped walking and Austin set me back on the ground. Taking two Snickers bars out of his pocket, he broke one in half for Gramps and Megan, and broke a piece from the other one for me. It filled my whole beak, and I had to gulp it down. Eating candy in eagle form wasn't very much fun. I couldn't really taste it. Austin offered me another piece, but I refused it. They could enjoy it far more than I could. Maybe I could find some rotten fish down by the water. Fish tainted with cyanide or dynamite.

Suddenly I felt like crying. I was hungry and tired and sad. I wanted to walk along next to them as I used to, not waddle along behind them like a disjointed chicken. I wanted to be able to eat like a human, not peck like a bird. I wanted to sleep lying down on a cot, not perched on the floor some-where. It was hard to keep my spirits up, but I had to. We had an almost impossible task to do, and I wasn't even sure how or where to start. I couldn't let Austin and Megan know how hopeless I felt. I was the leader here, right? I had to act like one.

Finally we arrived at the beach.

"Look! The houseboat's here," said Austin.

I flew up to a low branch of the nearest tree to have a look.

The houseboat was moored at the end of the pier. The bottom of the houseboat looked like a boat with a point at the bow and a flat back at the stern. The house part was made of bamboo, shaped in a rectangle. A bamboo roof came to a point in the middle of the house and extended over the sides and each end to provide shade. Doors were cut into each end, and narrow windows let the air go through to keep the boat cool. A length of deck ran along each end of the houseboat, where people could sit. In the front, a long wooden table stood in the center of the deck, with lanterns burning at both ends. A small grill for cooking stood on one end of the table. On the other end sat a large jug of water with a spout on the bottom. Boxes of canned goods, pots and pans, and other supplies were stacked against the wall under the extension of the roof.

Austin, Megan, and Gramps walked toward the house-boat, their footsteps sounding hollow on the dock's wooden planking. I waddled along behind, hungry and tired. Delicious smells wafted out into the air. They climbed a short ladder and stepped over the side onto the deck of the houseboat.

"What's cooking?" I flew over the side and perched on the end of the table. Mom was standing next to a camp cooker, frying something that looked like tacos. Aunt Jo was cutting vegetables. Jake sat next to her, eating celery.

"I'll bet you guys are hungry," said Mom. "I noticed you didn't eat much at the feast." She handed Austin a plate and pointed to the rough-looking picnic table. "Take these and sit down. Have some cheese, too." She put a plate on the table for me and added a piece of cheese.

"How about a soda?" asked Gramps. He went to a cooler and took out some sodas. He handed them around for us to share. Austin poured some in a cup for me.

As everyone ate, I pecked at the food on my plate. It was embarrassing to eat with a beak when everyone one else was picking the tacos up with their hands. I had to hold my head back and gulp the food down instead of chewing it like everyone else was doing. Next time I'd ask Mom to put my plate on the deck at the back of the boat so no one could watch.

When everyone was finished, the others helped Mom and Aunt Jo put the food away. Then Mom told us where we would sleep. Mom, Aunt Jo, and Megan would sleep in the room near the front of the boat. Gramps and Mr. Gifford would sleep in the smaller room near the stern. Austin, Jake, and I would sleep in the ranger station's back room. The panda was already there, in a shed at the back of the hut. Jake had gone to check on him and make sure he was safe. The villagers had given the panda water and bamboo shoots they'd collected from a place up in the hills.

When Austin and I left the houseboat, Megan walked with us a short way.

"We'll help get more bamboo shoots for the panda tomorrow," I said. "Then we need to try to find the cave."

"We'll meet in the morning for breakfast first," said Megan. "Don't get any ideas about leaving without me."

"We won't," said Austin. "Just bring along some extra food in case we're out there for a while. Mom got some groceries. See if you can pack a few things for us to take tomorrow."

"Your wish, my command." Megan's tone was indignant.

"I mean please do all that. Sorry." Austin sounded humble. "Do you want me to come and get the food?"

"No. You'd be too noisy. I'll do it. We don't want anyone to know what we're planning." She tiptoed away.

***

It was a long night. The panda was asleep in the shed, curled up in a ball. I tried to go to sleep too, but I wasn't used to sleeping while perching on a mat. Each time I started to drop off to sleep, a whiffling snore from the panda would jerk me awake. Finally I let my head rest backwards and slightly sideways against my neck feathers, and fell asleep.

Sometime later I heard a commotion outside. I waddled to the door and stared into the darkness. Austin heard it too. He pushed himself up from the bunk, and we went outside to have a look.

"Wait for me," I whispered. "I can check it out and tell you what's going on." I flew to the top of a nearby palm tree and settled on a strong branch. The moon was bright on the water, lighting the white-crested waves that rolled up onto the shore. Another big fishing boat had just tied up to the side of the pier, opposite the houseboat. Our people on the houseboat were awake too. Two figures crouched on the back deck. One was Gramps, and the other was Mr. Gifford. They kept their heads down. There were no lights on in the houseboat, but I was pretty sure Mom, Aunt Jo, and Megan were also awake. They'd probably stay down out of sight and listen.

Austin had climbed partway up the tree. I flew down and told him what was going on, then went back to my perch.

Captain Morrison, Mr. Burnell, and seven other men climbed down the rope ladder that hung over the side of the fishing boat. The myna bird perched on the cook's shoulder. For once Maggie was quiet. Even the bird seemed to realize that our lives had changed in the instant that Jake went crocodile on steroids.

My throat tightened when I saw the last man climb down. I hadn't seen his face since those terrible nights at the zoo. I'd never forget his evil grin when he zapped me with that cattle prod. Or the same evil grin when he shot its painful electrical rays into my brother. Dunn Nikowski was the stuff of nightmares. Now he was here with us again, on Komodo Island, where his actions had caused the curse that affected us all. Dunn Nikowski had caused the hole in the Whole.

The group moved quietly further inland, walking toward the tree where Austin and I were hiding. The crewmen looked frightened and nervous. The myna stared up at the top of the tree. Its beady dark eyes drilled into mine.

"Man overboard," squawked the myna. "Give us a kiss!"

"Shut up, you stupid bird," growled Dunn. "You'll have the whole camp awake."

"She's seen something," said Mr. Burnell. "I'd better take a look around. Somebody could be watching us."

He started down the path to the Rangers' Station, glancing right and left. Then he turned around and walked back, looking behind the trees. Thankfully he didn't look up or he would have seen Austin.

Burnell and the rest of the crew would have seen the

eagle on the turtle's back. They must have known something strange was going on. They might have missed the huge dolphin landing on the boat because it was gray like the deck. But they couldn't have missed the enormous Jake-crocodile when it slithered up out of the big square trap door onto the deck. That croc had morphed into the size of a two-trailer semi. They must have heard the crash when the croc's tail hit the big crane and knocked it down—and then the fight between the hippo and the croc. Maybe Dunn had paid them off to keep their mouths shut. But no wonder they looked so wary now. Some of the men probably believed Jake was magical or a demon. They had that right. Jake might have inherited some of his grandfather's traits.

Gramps probably wouldn't agree. He always said there was a little bad in the best of us and a little good in the worst of us. Dunn had caused the curse, stung us with the cattle-prod, and nearly killed us several times. And he still wanted more power. I didn't see even a smidgen of good in that man. Jake had done many cruel and terrible things. But now it seemed that Jake was sorry for the things he'd done. He was so sorry he didn't want to get off the sinking ship. Dunn wasn't sorry for anything. Jake seemed to like the panda and had offered to take care of it. He was beginning to be nicer to his mother, too. There did seem to be a little good in Jake Parma.

"Let's go back," said Dunn. His voice startled me. He and the cook were only a few yards from the tree where I was perched. "The rangers sleep in that hut over there. We don't want them up asking questions."

I watched them walk back to the beach. Two crewmembers climbed to the back of the fishing boat, hung over the stern, and untied the lifeboat. Walking with the rope in hand, they dragged it past the larger boat and up onto the sand. It looked as though they were going to sleep on the sand until morning. Captain Morrison handed the captain of the fishing boat some money. I could hear what they were saying.

"This is for picking us up," said Captain Morrison. "If you can pick us up the day after tomorrow and take us to Jakarta, we'll give you three times this much."

Dunn stepped forward and spoke to the captain of the fishing boat that had rescued them. "Mr. Brownlee, will you have enough room for the cages?"

Brownlee scratched his head. I couldn't see his face clearly, but his voice sounded worried. "Cages? What cages?"

"I already told you," growled Dunn. "We'll have a Komodo dragon and maybe a panda with us when we sail to Jakarta. I don't know for sure about the panda. I don't know if it made it here alive."

Mr. Brownlee held up his hands in alarm. "No! No Komodos on my boat. It could get out of the cage and eat us!"

"We'll get one that's already been fed." Dunn's droll tone of voice made it sound like being worried was stupid. "Don't worry. I'll pay you well."

Brownlee shook his head. "How can you pay me? You have nothing but the clothes you wear."

"I'll get money from my bank account," said Dunn. "I can call the bank when we get to Jakarta."

Brownlee shook his head. "First you get money, then we'll talk." He climbed back into his boat where two men waited for him. One of the men pulled up an anchor and the other started the engine. The big boat pulled away, leaving a path of choppy waves behind them.

Jake was up too. He must have been watching for his grandfather. His shoulders were slumped and he seemed to be having trouble putting one foot in front of the other, but he joined the men. Dunn was talking to the cook about a place to sleep. The cook knew someone in the village who had a big shed. He'd let men bunk down there for a couple of days and it wouldn't cost much.

"Hi, Grandpa," said Jake. "I'm glad you made it."

"Be ready to work in the morning, boy," said Dunn. "We have to build more crates."

Jake looked toward the crewmembers on the beach. "Will they have any food, Grandpa?"

"I don't know," said Dunn. "We'll see about food in the morning."

"Okay." Jake sounded sleepy and discouraged. He'd only picked at his food at supper. He was probably hungry.

Dunn and Mr. Burnell went on toward the village. The myna rode on the cook's shoulder, still quiet. Jake was several yards behind them. When he passed us, I called to him in a low voice.

"Jake, wait a minute."

Jake's head jerked around. "Who is that?"

"Us," said Austin, stepping out onto the path. "Mom said we're supposed to sleep in the ranger station's back room. You're supposed to sleep there too." Jake glanced at the two men, who were now too far away to call without waking someone.

Austin felt in his pockets. "One candy bar left." He held it out to Jake.

"Thanks." Jake stared at the candy bar in his hand. "Why did you give me this? It's your last one."

"You're hungry," said Austin.

"People aren't usually this nice to me," said Jake.

Austin and I glanced at each other. Jake hadn't been treated very well by his father or by his grandfather. He didn't believe his mother had been forced to leave him. He thought she'd just abandoned him. It was no wonder he couldn't believe that anyone would ever be kind to him.

We went into the hut. The rangers told us to take the back room, where three bamboo mats had been placed on the floor for us. The panda was in the shed, curled up in a corner. Someone had shoveled out the manure and scrubbed the floor.

Jake smiled when he saw the panda. "Can I sleep in here? I'll take care of him if you want."

"Okay by me." Austin went out the door and down the steps, back to the room where we were supposed to sleep. Jake lay down on the floor next to the panda and put one hand on the panda's leg. I stared at them for a few minutes. When we were at camp, Jake had pinched me until my arms and back were black and blue. He'd knocked me down in the shower, causing me to cut my head. He'd gotten three other guys to help tackle me, piling on top of me so that I couldn't breathe. He'd deliberately swamped Megan's canoe and nearly drowned her. He'd been a bully who didn't like anyone.

But he really liked the panda. He'd helped me save the animal's life when the ship was sinking, risking his own life in the process. Maybe that was the one good thing about Jake—he liked animals. If he liked animals, maybe he could learn to like people, too.

I went outside and flew into the Rangers' Station, then through the door to the back room. I perched on the floor next to Austin's mat and closed my eyes. There were still a few hours until morning. A cool breeze came in through the window. I lifted my head and stretched my wings to let the air blow through my feathers. I longed to lie down on my bamboo mat and put my head on a pillow, but I couldn't. Eagles don't sleep that way, and I didn't want to use either of my other forms in the ranger's hut. My eyes felt gritty. I closed them and tried to relax. A cloud wafted across the moon, and a soft gray darkness fell around me. My head fell back a little and I surrendered to sleep. The next thing I knew, sunshine was glowing through the window and streaming across the hard floor of the hut. It was morning.

Chapter Eight—Nemesis

I stretched my neck, making the feathers stand up off my skin. Then I flapped my wings a few times and scanned the room. Austin was sitting up, stretching. I checked the shed. The panda was sitting up too, watching us. The water pan was full. Jake must have gotten the water for it before he left. Where was Jake now?

I followed Austin to the ocean, where the houseboat was moored, remembering to limp and drag my wing.

"We have to talk about today," I said, catching up with my brother. "While we're up there getting bamboo shoots, we need to keep an eye out for caves."

"That's going to be hard," said Austin. "The ranger probably won't let us leave the group."

"I can leave the group anytime I want." I darted into the air, circled him, and landed, all in about five seconds.

The odor of cooking meat wafted through the air as we neared the houseboat.

"Yum!" Austin and I said together. I flew over the side as Jake climbed the ladder and jumped onto the deck.

"Here are the boys." Mom glanced past Austin, then back to me. "Where's Jake?"

"He got up before we did," I said. "I don't know where he went."

"He's probably with his grandfather," said Austin. "I heard them arrive during the night." He lowered his head in my direction. "Luke, check out those guys who are talking to the rangers. Isn't that Dunn and Jake?"

I peered at them, focusing at about two hundred yards. It was Dunn, all right. My heart began thumping hard, just looking at him. Jake was walking next to him, fists clenched. He kicked a rock, sending it about twenty feet. I could hear them talking.

"I need you to help build cages today." Dunn's voice was harsh.

Jake stepped a little away from Dunn before he answered. "I can't, Gramps. I have things of my own to take care of."

Dunn reached out and grabbed him by the arm. "You'll do what I say."

I focused in on Jake. His face was flushed and his lips pressed tightly together. They were near the beach now, and we were only about thirty yards away, so we could see them clearly. Nearby, several pieces of wood had floated in to shore.

Mr. Burnell, the cook from the ship, was directing some men to pick up the wood and put it in a pile. He held up a piece of paper that had a picture on it. Focusing, I saw what was on the paper—a box with slats. It was a diagram of a crate.

"What are they doing?" whispered Austin.

"They're going to build a large crate," I answered. "Guess

what they'll put in it."

"I'm hungry, Gramps." Jake glanced toward the house-boat. He could probably smell the good cooking. "Do you have any food?"

"No, I don't. You can go find some if you want, but get back here in fifteen minutes."

Dunn's head bent toward the cook's as they talked about the design for the crate. Suddenly Dunn's head snapped up, and he stared straight ahead. His face was a mask of confusion, as though he suddenly couldn't remember his own name. He wrinkled his brow and his mouth dropped open. Though we were still several yards away, I heard the word he whispered.

"Katerie." He stared, open-mouthed, into the trees.

I followed his gaze. About twenty yards away, Megan's grandmother stood as still as a statue. Her eyes were wide and her hand covered her mouth, as though she had seen something shocking. The breeze lifted her hair and made her skirts billow and fall flat against her legs. Megan came running from the houseboat and stopped next to me. She reached for my hand, forgetting that I didn't have one. I touched her hand with the tip of my wing and left it there. From the side of my eye, I saw Austin take her other hand. We stood like that for several seconds, looking from Dunn to Katerie and back again.

Katerie began to walk toward Dunn. He tried to say something, but it came out in a stutter. He looked quickly from side to side, as though checking for an escape route. I could feel all the animals that he'd ever morphed into—even the huge crocodile—wanting to flee from the approaching woman.

As Katerie drew closer, Dunn stepped backwards. His

foot hit a tree root, and he tripped and fell. He sprawled awkwardly on the ground, struggling to get up. His right leg was flung out to the side, the knee bent in the wrong direction. He pushed up from his left leg, but the right one kept sliding out from under him. Jake bent to help him, but Dunn pushed him away. He shoved himself up from the ground again, swearing. Once again the right leg slipped, and Dunn landed on his back end in the dirt. The artificial leg must have detached somehow. It fell out of his trouser leg and lay there on the ground. I felt embarrassed for him, as though he'd lost his underwear or something. Dunn reached for the metal leg, his eyes bulging and his face almost purple. He looked so angry I half expected him to start foaming at the mouth.

Katerie hurried forward and sat down next to him in the dirt. Jake stared at the scene that unfolded before us. He glanced at Megan, his brow wrinkled. Megan shrugged in response, as if she didn't know what was going on either.

"I'll bet Jake has never seen that happen before," whispered Austin. "Maybe he didn't even know Dunn has an artificial leg."

Megan didn't answer. She stared straight ahead, her mouth slightly open.

"Don't move," said Katerie, as Dunn tried to crawl away from her. She made him turn back so his leg was extended toward her, then pushed his empty pant leg up to his thigh. We could see the white stump—the part of the leg that was left after the Komodo bit him all those years ago. I'd never seen a stump before, and it shocked me a little. The gash from the Komodo's bite had been so large that the doctor had to amputate most of Dunn's leg, taking it off about halfway between the knee and the thigh. A flap of skin had been sewn neatly over the bottom of the stump, leaving an old scar around its edges. It looked pale and odd, kind of like a white turkey breast sticking out of a pant leg.

Katerie had picked up the artificial leg and was brushing the dirt from it. I realized what Gramps always called a "tin leg" was just an expression. It was mostly made of strong steel. The top was a wide leather piece that would be fastened around the stump. Two pieces of steel extended from the leather, each attached to a movable metal circle. These circles acted as a knee joint, allowing the lower part of the artificial leg to bend. Beneath the knee circles was a short steel rod that ended in a molded foot. The foot would fit into a shoe. It must have taken a lot of practice for Dunn to learn to walk on it.

Katerie knew what to do. In seconds she'd laced and buckled the tin leg onto the stump. She pulled Dunn's trouser leg down to the foot and pushed the artificial foot into his shoe.

"You remembered," said Dunn, moving his leg back and forth. It looked fine. No one would guess what was under there.

Katerie stood up, dusting the front of her skirt. "I never forgot."

Dunn pushed himself up carefully until he was standing. He wobbled at first, signaling Jake for help. Jake hurried to Dunn's side, allowing his grandfather to hold onto him.

Katerie nodded toward the other leg. "I see you have two metal legs now. I suppose you couldn't keep out of trouble."

Dunn's face twisted into a smile. I glanced at Gramps. He stood there with his arms crossed, watching. He was probably thinking about that last battle in the zoo parking lot. Dunn hadn't lost his life, but he had lost his second leg. Though he'd been cruel to all of us, I couldn't help feeling bad for him. I had to use crutches once when I sprained an ankle. I could barely walk with those, and I had one good leg. It must have been really hard to learn to walk on two artificial legs.

"Dunn." Katerie waved a hand in our direction. "That girl is Megan, our granddaughter. She's Angelina's child. Megan looks like Angelina, doesn't she?"

Dunn glanced our way. I wanted to yell, *"This is the granddaughter you hid on the water tower at the zoo. Then you let her fall. She could have been killed!"* But I said nothing. This whole thing was Dunn's fault. The curse, these feathers that had ruined my life, all of it was because of him. For me this wasn't a social occasion. Dunn was our enemy, and the cause of all our trouble. If he hadn't provoked that Komodo all those years ago, just out of sheer meanness, it wouldn't have bitten him and Gramps wouldn't have had to shoot it. The medicine woman wouldn't have put a curse on Gramps, Dunn, and all their descendants. I wouldn't be standing here, thousands of miles from my home, trying to find a pink Komodo that might not even exist anymore.

Katerie walked toward us, holding out her hand to Megan. Megan let go of me and Austin and took her grandmother's hand. "Let's go see your grandfather," said Katerie. Megan pulled away, shaking her head.

"I'd rather not, Grandmother. He hasn't been very nice to me. Or to any of us."

Katerie looked deeply sad. "He's never very nice to anyone. Or anything." She didn't try to take Megan's hand again.

Dunn had already turned his back on Katerie and Megan and was heading toward the beach. He waved for Jake to come with him. Jake glanced at us, then back at his grandfather. I knew he didn't want to go. I flew along the beach and landed next to him. "Your mom will be looking for you, Jake. Come on."

He shook his head. "I doubt it. She doesn't care about me. Nobody does. I wreck everything, even when I don't mean to." He looked at me and Austin, who was walking toward us, and his voice choked. "I don't know why I went crocodile like that. I just felt like I was going to explode. And then I did."

I flapped my wings. "It's the wild boar still inside you, probably. They don't have much control. You'll be much better when we get rid of this curse."

"Maybe now you understand how your mother felt when she went wolf that first time," said Austin. "She didn't know what happened to her, either."

Jake was quiet then, staring at the sand. He looked sad. He was probably hungry too. I felt bad for him. I hated for people to be hungry.

"Hurry up!" yelled Dunn.

Jake followed him further up the beach. Several more pieces of wood had floated in with the tide. The crew and some of the men from the island were dragging the wood up onto the sand and laying it out to dry. They had laid some long pieces in the shape of a rectangle and were placing more boards across them, leaving space between them. I knew what they were doing. They were building a large, wooden box with slats.

I shivered as I stared at the makeshift crate. Dunn was going to go on with his plan to catch a Komodo and sell it to a zoo. But not any Komodo. I'd heard him say the pink one would be worth thousands of dollars. He'd also said he didn't care if it died, just so we didn't get it. He knew we were trying to undo the curse.

Dunn wanted to keep the curse going. He wanted to have the power to grow into huge, vicious animals anytime he wanted. He wanted people and other animals to be afraid of him and do whatever he said. The rest of us had only used our animal forms for self-defense and to protect others. Dunn and Jake used their forms to gain power and hurt people. Now they were going to try to keep us from finding the pink Komodo. It was up to me to make sure this didn't happen. Austin, Megan, and Gramps would help, but I would have to tell them what to do.

We went to the houseboat to eat breakfast. Megan and Austin climbed up the ladder and I flew over the side. All the adults were up. Gramps was making pancakes, and Aunt Jo was making instant coffee and cocoa. There was instant cereal too, and cans of orange juice. We needed a good breakfast this morning. We had a lot to do and we needed energy. First we would go up into the hills where the bamboo shoots grew and help bring several piles down for the panda. Then Austin, Megan, and I would try to find the cave where the pink Komodo lived.

A new ranger stopped in to greet us. "I'm Madeline Crawford," she said, shaking our hands. "Call me Maddie."

Megan's eyes grew wide, and her face glowed with admiration. She held out her hand to the ranger. "Nice to meet you." Maddie shook Megan's hand.

"A woman ranger," said Megan. "Of course there would be. I just never thought of it."

"That's understandable," said Maddie. "It's a hard life. You have to be strong and be able to get along without a lot of creature comforts."

"You mean like going without food and sleeping on palm leaves?" asked Megan.

"I mean like going without indoor plumbing and going for days without any clean clothes," said Maddie.

She spoke English with an accent I'd heard before. Michigan was right over the border from Canada. Mom and Dad had taken us to Canada on vacation. I wished I could talk to Maddie, to find out if she was Canadian.

"It must be a wonderful career, or you wouldn't be here, right?" Megan sat on the bench that was built along the boat's deck and waited. If she'd had any paper, I was sure she'd be taking notes. I had questions too, but I didn't dare ask them. This pretty ranger thought I was an eagle, and she'd be shocked if she heard me talk. So I stayed quiet and listened.

Maddie listed all the things rangers did on Komodo Island. A lot of it had to do with conservation. "We try to find the burrows where they lay their eggs," said Maddie. "We want to protect those eggs if we can. The number of Komodos decreases every year. We think there are only about two thousand left on the three islands in Indonesia where they've been found. Komodos live here, and on Flores and Rinca, our neighboring islands. They aren't found anywhere else in the world. It's been such a privilege to see them." She patted Megan's hand. "So yes, it is a wonderful career. But it's not for everyone."

"You must know the island pretty well," said Austin. "Do you go up there a lot?" He gestured toward the hills that blended into the chain of gray mountains.

"I've been to some places, but not all over the entire island. I've gone around it, but not that far up into the mountains. It's dangerous, and we have so much work to do here that there really isn't time." Maddie eyed Austin, and then Megan. "We don't encourage tourists to go up there either. The guides can't protect you from an attack. They carry those sticks, but a hungry Komodo would just bite it in half and then go after you."

"We saw a couple at the feast yesterday," said Austin. "The men chased them away with those sticks."

When Maddie laughed, dimples appeared in her cheeks and her blue eyes sparkled. "The natives keep them well fed, so they're too lazy to hunt. They aren't really that hungry or they wouldn't be so easily distracted." She pointed toward the mountains. "Up there, the Komodos have to hunt. And remember, they are the lead predator in this area."

Megan frowned. "What does that mean?"

"It means they're the top of the food chain," Austin answered. "So we're on their list of prey."

"Maddie, have you ever seen a pink Komodo?" Megan's voice was hopeful.

"Once," said the ranger. "It was at a zoo in Jakarta."

Megan hung her head. "So we don't even know that there is another one."

I bit back the words I wanted to say and screeched instead.

Maddie narrowed her eyes. "What's the matter with that eagle? I see it's dragging one wing."

"I think it's hurt," said Austin. "We keep it with us to protect it."

"We have a panda with us too," added Megan.

Maddie's eyebrows went up. "A panda? Where on earth did you get it?"

"He was already on the ship when we boarded," Austin explained. "When the ship sank, we managed to save him."

Maddie huffed out a breath. "Wow! Of course the animal will need food. We'll go up in the hills, where there's a bamboo forest. The people here use bamboo to make lots of things. I'll take a look at your panda before we leave to make sure he doesn't need a vet or additional care."

Maddie left to examine the panda while we waited.

The rangers brought us bottles of water. They agreed that Maddie could take us to the place where the bamboo grew. They found two men from the village, who would go with us to cut it down. When we were at the feast, Austin had bought several cloth sacks from a woman who made them to sell to tourists. He gave one to each person in the group, except me, of course. Into the bags my friends loaded water bottles and some of the snack bars Mom had asked Captain Miklos to get with the grocery order. Megan had the extra food for the three of us in her backpack. Austin carried my supply of water with his. He also took the rope he'd purchased from Captain Miklos.

When Maddie returned we set out, walking single file on the trail that led up the hill to the bamboo forest. I flew low, gliding back and forth over them. I landed occasionally to keep up the pretense that I was lame.

"What did you think about the panda?" asked Austin.

"She appears dehydrated and undernourished," said Maddie.

"She?" Megan's eyes widened.

Maddie laughed. "The panda is female. The villagers are bringing her water and bamboo shoots. I think she'll be okay in a few days."

Megan walked next to Maddie, chattering and questioning her about a research project she was doing. Jake, Mr. Gifford, and Gramps came too. I was surprised to see Jake. His grandfather had told him to help build crates.

We'd only walked a few minutes when we saw Dunn standing in the middle of the trail. He held his hand out like a traffic cop.

"Get out of that line, boy," Dunn snapped. "We've got work to do."

"He's coming with us," said Gramps. "I'm responsible for him. If you interfere, you'll be talking to a judge when we go back." He handed Jake a sack with water and other supplies. "Stay next to me, Jake."

Maddie watched all this, frowning. "Is there a problem here?"

"No problem," said Gramps.

"You'll have the devil to pay when you get back, boy," Dunn shouted.

"Don't worry, Jake." Gramps turned to Dunn. "If you threaten Jake again or even say one cross word to him, I'll see you in court when we get back. Got that?"

I felt my beak cracking as I tried to grin. I loved hearing Gramps get tough with Dunn. Gramps turned to Jake. "Don't worry, son. We won't let him hurt you."

"We'll all protect you," said Mr. Gifford.

"That's right," said Austin. "Just wait until Dunn meets your mother in full howl."

Jake laughed. I'd never heard him laugh before. I didn't trust Dunn, though. He might do something to get back at us.

"Gramps," I whispered. "Mom and Aunt Jo are down there alone. Do you think they'll be okay? Dunn is pretty mad."

"You're right," said Gramps. "Maybe I should go back."

"I'll go with you," said Mr. Gifford. "You kids stick together and stay with the ranger. We'll see you later." He turned to his nephew. "Don't worry, Jake. We'll keep Dunn under control."

They turned to go back down the path. It made me feel better to know Mom and Aunt Jo wouldn't be alone. Austin and I both knew what Dunn could do if he wanted to be mean.

Jake had stopped on the path and was staring back at the village. Dunn was almost out of sight now. "Maybe I should go back," he said. "I don't know what my grandfather will do. He's had some bad ideas—things that hurt people."

"We know all about him, Jake. We all fought him at the zoo," said Austin. "He did every mean thing you could possibly imagine."

"And some you probably can't imagine," added Megan. She touched her cousin's arm. "Don't worry. Dr. Kenwood and Uncle Roy will help if there's a problem."

"I know." Jake narrowed his eyes and reached a hand toward Megan's neck. It was bruised, and there was a swollen, reddened line along one side. "I did that, didn't I, when I grabbed the necklace. I'm so sorry." He shook his head and stared at the ground. "Grandfather told me to get it, but that's no excuse. You probably can't forgive me, and I don't blame you."

Megan left her hand on his arm and gave a slight smile. "I'm sure you didn't know it was going to bruise my neck like this. And I'm sure you won't do anything like this again."

He swallowed hard, and shook his head. "No. Never again. I'm really, really sorry."

"Then let's forget it," said Megan.

Jake smiled at her. It was the second time I'd seen him smile. A real smile, not like the nasty sneers he gave me at camp. He'd just laughed, too. Then he actually apologized to Megan. Jake seemed a lot nicer since he'd been taking care of the panda. I hoped it would last.

Chapter Nine—Mairghread and Roux

After Gramps and Mr. Gifford left, Maddie talked to us about the Komodo dragons.

"Komodo Island and the other islands where Komodos still live are now part of Komodo National Park. As I told you yesterday, there are only about two thousand left, and they are considered endangered. No one may hunt or capture one without special permission."

That made me happy. I thought about the big crate that had been down on Level Five of the cargo ship—the crate with the heart symbol with a small hole in the center. The ship had taken that crate down with it. But right now Dunn and some of the men were building another crate. He still meant to capture a Komodo and try to sell it to a zoo. I was glad to learn that hunting the Komodos was illegal. Maddie said regular patrols were carried out to enforce these laws. If I couldn't stop Dunn from capturing the pink Komodo, maybe the rangers could.

Megan was walking in the grass so she could talk to Maddie. "I wanted to hear more about your research study," said Megan.

"We could talk about that more when we get back to camp, Megan. Then your friends can hear too."

"Oh, they aren't interested," said Megan. I let out a squawk.

"We all want to hear," said Austin.

"When we get back, we'll get some sodas from the ranger station, and I'll be glad to tell anyone who wants to hear about it," said Maddie. She stopped at a nearby tree and reached for a piece of fruit that hung from a thick twig. It was an oval, flattish green fruit about six inches long. "This is a jackfruit." She held it up so everyone could see it. "We had some of this with our pork yesterday. Mango and coconuts grow on trees here too. There are several mango trees near the village."

The group walked single file, staying on a well-worn path that led up the hill. I flew off, circling slowly overhead. I scanned the area, watching for Komodos. With their coloring, they blended into rocky areas. I didn't want anyone to startle a Komodo into attacking. I saw one long gray Komodo just ahead, basking in the sun in a shallow, scooped out place. I landed behind Austin. He bent down to me.

"Komodo just ahead," I whispered. "On the right about thirty yards from the path."

Austin nodded. We both knew we could protect the group if the Komodo attacked, but we didn't want to have to morph in front of the ranger or the men from the village. Hopefully the huge creature wasn't hungry. It didn't seem to be hunting; it was just lying there.

The heat was pressing in on us. The hikers paused to have a drink from their water bottles. I was getting very thirsty too, but I couldn't drink from a bottle because of my beak. Austin didn't forget me. He took a cup from his backpack and poured water in it for me to drink. Despite the heat a breeze was coming off the ocean, and that felt good. I flew into the air for a few minutes to catch the cool air in my wings.

"I've been watching for Komodo dragons," said Jake.

"Look right over there," said Maddie. "There's one in that long gully. Sometimes they lay their eggs in gullies. They also use shallow caves or other protected areas."

"Do the mother Komodos protect the babies?" asked Megan.

"Younger Komodos climb up into trees as soon as they hatch," said Maddie. "Otherwise the older ones will eat them. One scientist saw a mother komodo stand guard while the hatchlings ran to the trees, but usually the babies have to make it on their own."

After we'd walked about another mile, we saw the bamboo forest. They were sturdy, woody looking plants, some of them as tall and thick as trees. Maddie stopped in the middle of a large bunch of bamboo plants.

"People come up here and cut these down." She pointed to some thicker trees. "They use the bamboo to build huts, furniture, or cut it into slices to make baskets and many other items. You can buy things made from bamboo in the village. Our people need the money they earn to buy food, medicine, and things they can't make."

Behind and between the thick bamboo trees, I saw lots of new, skinny shoots with leaves sprouting from the top. I whispered to Austin that we should cut those for the panda.

"I've seen pictures of pandas eating bamboo shoots," said Austin. "They looked more like these skinny plants."

"Let's cut these and take some back. It's the best we can do for the panda right now," said Maddie.

"Are these the same as the bamboo shoots that grow in China?" asked Austin.

"Probably similar, but I'm no expert," said Maddie. "There are several varieties. Bamboo is found in many Asian countries with similar climates." She spoke to the men from the village who had come with us. "Please cut the thin shoots, with leaves and twigs. We'll put them in piles to carry back to the panda."

While they were busy with the bamboo, I soared further up the hill to the lowest part of the mountains. The Elder had told us that the pink Komodo could be found in a cave where the hills met the mountain. I flew along the gray ridge of mountain that sprang up from the grass, watching for holes or slits in the rock that could open into a cave. From the air I could see dark openings, but I couldn't see inside them. I couldn't be sure an opening led into a cave unless I actually landed and took a closer look.

The group on the ground was busy gathering bamboo shoots into piles. Soon they'd be ready to pick up the piles and go back to the village. I didn't have much time. I flew lower, gliding along the mountainside for another quarter mile. Then I saw something that made my heart jump. There, carved into the side of the mountain, was the shape of a heart. Inside the heart was a small, round circle. It was the same symbol we carried on our bracelets, and the same symbol Katerie had drawn on her letters to Megan. This had to be the place the Elder was talking about! I landed with a thump, digging my talons into the dirt.

"You have been a long time coming."

The voice came from somewhere behind the rock. I was so startled I nearly shed some of my feathers. My heart pounded. I was scared, but I didn't fly away. The symbol on the rock meant I had found something important. The person who had spoken seemed to have been waiting for me. I felt sure I was supposed to be here. Stumbling along on my talons, I saw a flat piece of rock propped up against the side of the mountain. Behind it an opening led into a dark space. Taking a deep breath, I noticed the faint smell of pine in the air, but there were no pine trees in the area. I peered inside.

"Do not be afraid. Come in." It was the voice of a woman. I waddled past the slab of rock and into the dim space. The only light came from outside. I moved forward, balancing on my talons. Soon I could see a woman's shape, sitting on a rock.

She struck a match. In the light of the small flame, I saw the woman's hand light a candle and raise it toward her face as she blew the match out. She was old, much older than Gramps, but her face was wise and kindly. Her hair was long and white, and her skirt flowed down to her feet.

She held the burning candle high, and the cave came alight with color. What I saw took my breath away. Behind her, a huge Komodo dragon lay with its head on the ground, its eyes closed. In the soft glow of the candle, the Komodo's body gleamed like pink armor, the color flowing up and down as it breathed. I let out a small gasp as I stared at the vision before me. I could hardly believe it was real. The pink Komodo was here, lying right in front of me! I blinked, then blinked again to make sure I wasn't seeing things. I wanted to reach out and touch it, but then I remembered I had no hands. For now, all I could do was gaze at it in wonder.

"My name is Luke. Luke Brockway," I said. My voice was

hoarse from the feeling of excitement. "I'm not really an eagle."

"You are welcome, Luke Brockway," said the woman. "In your language, my name would be Mairghread." I was still staring at the pink Komodo.

"Her name is Roux," said Mairghread. It was the same name the Elder had mentioned.

"Nice to meet you both." I tried to be polite, but I felt stunned. I'd just met the medicine woman, the very one who put the curse on Gramps and Dunn. And here was the pink Komodo, huge and looking almost magical in the dim light of the cave.

Now something else caught my attention. Beyond the Komodo, the wall of the cave was alive with colorful drawings. People placing palm leaves filled with food in front of a pink Komodo. Gray Komodos chasing wild pigs. Figures with raised spears who appeared to be hunting. Two men carrying a wild pig hanging upside down from a pole. Mothers with babies on their backs. People sitting around fires that lit the darkness. Women cooking in front of huts with circular bamboo roofs.

Mairghread walked behind me with the candle so I could see. Following the pictures, I toddled along the back wall of the cave. Some person, or persons, had kept a history of their people, documented in their drawings. The last drawing, bigger than the others, was of a pink Komodo. It lay motionless on the ground, its forked tongue hanging sideways from its open mouth. A man stood in front of it, holding a gun. Next to him another man lay on the ground. His leg was bloody, and half of it was missing.

My neck feathers ruffled as I shivered beneath them. With the tip of my wing, I pointed to the last painting. "Is this... is this..." I couldn't get the words out. The impact of what had happened here all those years ago flooded over me, heavy and sad. I was looking at a drawing of my own grandfather and the pink Komodo he'd shot to save Dunn Nikowski's life. That was Dunn on the ground, his leg half missing. That was the last drawing. The span of rock after it was gray and clean. It was as if the history of the island people had stopped with the death of the pink Komodo. I stood there awed by it, trembling beneath my feathers.

Mairghread moved her head slightly, as if watching for someone else to come into the cave. "I've heard that your grandfather is here. What about the other one? The one who married my daughter?" Her eyes were bright, watching me.

"Dunn Nikowski? He got here last night. We had some trouble." I told her about the shipwreck and how we used our animal forms to protect everyone. I told her about Austin and Megan, who had saved us. Suddenly I felt very lonely. Austin and Megan should be here. We'd come all this way together. They deserved to see this. Besides, Mairghread was Megan's great-grandmother. As soon as I could, I would fly out and get them. But first I needed to talk to the medicine woman while I had the chance. I had to find out how to remove the curse.

"Megan, your great-granddaughter, was very brave," I said. "She turned into a giant sea turtle and carried us on her back for many miles. You will be proud of her."

The medicine woman smiled and nodded. "Yes. Angelina's daughter. She has our blood. She will be medicine woman when Katerie dies."

My beak fell open. Another shock wave of emotion made my feathers quake. What if Megan didn't want to be a medicine woman? She would have to live on this island for the rest of her life. The island was beautiful, but we were used to so many other things. We had nice schools and sports teams. Megan played soccer, and she was really good at it. We could go to movies and eat hamburgers or have hot fudge sundaes at restaurants. She was already talking about going to college. Would she be willing to give all that up to live here and follow in Katerie's footsteps?

The medicine woman chuckled. "I can see your heart pounding right through those feathers, Luke Brockway. You are her friend. You are worried about her. Don't be. My great-granddaughter may choose the life of a medicine woman or she may not choose it. It's up to her."

My chest feathers relaxed. I tried to imagine Megan as medicine woman here on Komodo Island. It wasn't hard. She liked to help people and she was very smart. It would make me sad if she stayed here, though. She was a good friend. I would miss her. I decided not to mention this to Austin.

"We need your help," I said. I explained what Gramps had told us about undoing the curse. "I don't mean to complain, but I'm really tired of being an eagle. I can't change back to human form. I've tried and tried, and nothing works. It's hard to eat or drink. I'm thirsty all the time. I can't lie down to sleep." I sighed. "Sorry. I'm complaining a lot."

She reached out to touch the feathers on my wings. "This is too much of a burden for one so young to bear."

"My grandfather said we must find the pink Komodo and return it to the people of Komodo Island. But you already have her. What else must we do?"

"You must repair the hole in the Whole," she answered. When she said "Whole" she moved her arms to make a large circle, just as the Elder had done the day before. I still didn't understand what he meant. Now the medicine woman was telling me the same thing. I didn't understand her either.

The medicine woman took her seat on the flat rock and patted the place next to her. "Sit here," she said. I flew up to perch next to the place where she sat.

"My grandfather believes this is all his fault," I told her. "He believes he created that hole you're talking about when he shot the Komodo. He says that's why we're all cursed."

"Your grandfather is wrong," said the medicine woman. "He didn't cause the curse. It started with the first disturbance of the Komodo by Dunn. He was the one who caused the hole in the Whole."

She waved her arm again, taking in the cave around us. "We are all connected by the great fabric of the universe," said the medicine woman. "Our energy is linked by waves that no one can see. But they are real. When one person hurts another, or hurts a creature, or harms the earth, it causes damage to this invisible web. It causes a hole..." She made a circle with her thumb and finger. "... in the Whole." She again made a great circle with her arms.

The sleeping dragon stirred. My feathers prickled. The pink Komodo was pretty, but it was still a Komodo dragon. If it wanted to, it could swallow me in two bites. The Komodo opened its eyes and turned its head toward me. It flicked its tongue, tasting the air. I shivered, hoping the medicine woman had fed it.

Mairghread turned toward the Komodo and ran her hand along the pink scales as though comforting it. The Komodo's chest rose and fell as it took a deep breath. Its rosy scales glittered in the flickering candlelight. Lowering her head, Roux closed her eyes again, and the medicine woman continued her story.

"Before Dunn and your grandfather visited, only a few people came to see the Komodos. Mostly they were people who wanted to study them. They were respectful to us and to the animals. They didn't disturb them or the island." The medicine woman held out her hand toward the sleeping Komodo. "Then your grandfather and Dunn Nikowski came to the island. Dunn hit Roux's mother and hurt her. She did what Komodos do to defend themselves. She bit Dunn's leg. She might have gone on eating him if your grandfather hadn't been there. He shot her to save Dunn's life."

I nodded toward the painting on the wall. "Is that my grandfather with the gun, and Dunn with the bloody leg?" I knew it was, but I wanted to hear what she would say about it.

Mairghread sighed. "Yes. That is the story of our people. Through the years, more and more pictures appeared. No one knows who painted them. After Roux's mother was shot, the artists must have lost heart. Nothing else has been painted on the wall since then."

I nodded. I was sorry about the paintings, but I had more important things to worry about, like getting rid of these feathers. "If it was Dunn's fault, why did Gramps have to be cursed too? And all of us?"

She lifted her shoulders and waved her hand toward the cave entrance. "Your grandfather saved Dunn's life, but after that he did not try to help. He told Katerie he had to get back to his ship. Dunn stayed, but he did not help repair the damage." She sighed, staring at the floor. "After that happened, things began to change here. More and more people came to our islands to see the Komodos. Sometimes they hunted and killed them. Some of them captured Komodos for zoos and took them away without asking. They bought our fish and the things we made from bamboo, giving us money. Our people grew used to this. Some of them became greedy. For years our people took just enough fish from the ocean for themselves and their families. But as more visitors came, they used dynamite and other explosives to get bigger catches and make more money. Their dynamite killed many ocean species and damaged the coral reefs. The beautiful reefs will never recover. The Komodos were disturbed by the blasting. They didn't lay as many eggs and their numbers decreased."

As I listened to her, I became more and more alarmed. She was talking about problems Austin, Megan, and I couldn't possibly solve. If that was what it would take to remove the curse, we wouldn't be able to do it! I would be trapped in these feathers forever!

"These problems are happening all over the world," I cried. "We've learned a lot about it in school. I don't know how we can stop it." I hung my feathered head. "I'm going to be an eagle forever. There's nothing I can do to fix the hole in the Whole." I stretched my wings on the word "Whole." "It's become too big for us to mend!"

"Be calm," said Mairghread. Smiling, she touched my wing again. "You don't have to solve all the problems. Only do what is yours to do."

"Do what is ours to do? What does that mean?" I blinked at her, fearing the answer.

"If you and your friends protect Roux and her eggs, it will be enough to undo the curse. Keep Roux from being taken or killed. Protect her eggs, too, if you can."

I let out a long breath, feeling a weight removed from my feathered shoulders. Between the three of us, we should be able to protect this Komodo.

"Do I have to stay in eagle form until then? The others became human again. It's so hard to live in this form. I'm so thirsty."

"I didn't choose the eagle, Luke. You did. If I take the eagle form from you now, you might not be able to use it again when you need it." She rose and picked up the candle. "Come with me." The smell of pine and bayberry wafted in the air as she moved.

The Komodo snorted, but she didn't open her eyes. I flew over her and landed at the back corner of the cave. A small stream of water trickled through the rock and down into a small pool on the floor. Reaching down, Mairghread took a bowl from the side of the pool and held it under the stream. "Drink," she said, placing the water in front of me. I dipped my beak into the bowl and drank. The water was cold and sweet. I drank for a long time, pecking and swallowing, pecking and swallowing some more. Soon I felt better.

"You said we must protect the pink Komodo's eggs," I said. The medicine woman nodded. I surveyed the cave, from the floor to every crevice. "Where are the eggs? I don't see them."

Mairghread waved her arm. "There," she said. "Next to the flowing stream."

I walked to the place she was pointing at. Behind the rock where the stream was flowing I saw another narrow opening. Keeping my wings folded, I waddled through it. The inner cave was smaller than the outer room, and I didn't see any openings to the outside. The water streamed from somewhere above me and through a space above the rock to the outer cave.

Scanning the floor of gray rock, I found what I was looking for. Seven eggs lay in a narrow depression next to the back wall. These eggs were precious. They were Roux's eggs. She was the special Komodo, the guardian of the island. All we had to do was protect Roux and her eggs. It seemed easy enough. Roux was sleeping peacefully in the outer cave, and the medicine woman was with her. The eggs were hidden here, in this little inner cave. Kneeling next to the eggs, I examined each of them carefully. They were not cracked or damaged or dirty. With my acute Komodo hearing, I thought I could hear movement. Perhaps they were nearly ready to hatch. That would be exciting! I couldn't wait to see the babies.

I slid back through the narrow opening and found Mairghread waiting for me at the entrance to the cave.

"Go now," said the medicine woman. "Your friends will be worried about you."

"They'll be so excited to hear that I've met you," I said. "I can't wait to tell them!"

Mairghread shook her head. "You mustn't tell anyone that you've seen me. It must be our secret. If you bring your friends here, you must make sure no one knows—and you must not speak of having been here before."

What was she saying? I couldn't believe my ears.

"What about my grandfather? Can't I even tell him?"

She shook her head. "No, not even him. You see, there are people everywhere. It's as if the very trees have ears. When you tell even a single person, someone will hear. Soon Dunn will know where I am. He will know where she is." She touched the sleeping Komodo gently. "Dunn will try to take her," said the medicine woman.

"That's true," I said. "He thinks he can get thousands of

dollars for her."

"She's old," said the medicine woman. "She would die from stress from being captured."

"He won't care if she dies. I heard him say that myself. He doesn't want us to undo the curse. He wants to keep it. He likes the power he has when he grows into large animals."

Mairghread stared at the floor, shaking her head. "That would do even more damage to the fabric of our world. It will make such a big tear in the Whole that we may never be able to fix it." She fixed her eyes on me, and I couldn't look away. "Promise me," she said, putting her hand on my feathery head. "You must not tell anyone that you've seen me, or that you've found the pink Komodo. Dunn will hear, and he could get to her first."

With a sinking feeling in my chest, I promised not to tell anyone about finding Mairghread or the Komodo.

"I promise you this in return, Luke Brockway," she said, smiling. "You will be human again. And very soon."

I said goodbye and flew back to the bamboo forest. The piles of bamboo were gone. Gramps, Austin, Megan, and the others were nowhere in sight. Flying low, I followed the trail back towards the ranger's hut. I soon spotted my group, about a mile ahead. Maddie and Megan were leading them. Austin was near the back. When he saw me, he waved his arms and yelled something to the others. I landed next to him. The others were watching, so I limped a little.

"Where have you been?" whispered Austin. "I was worried that something had happened to you." He put down his bag of bamboo shoots and took a drink of his water.

"I was looking for the cave the Elder told us about. I was also looking for fresh water."

A drop of water rolled down the side of Austin's bottle. I poked at it with my beak. I didn't want him to ask me any more questions about where I'd been, so I tried to make him think I was still thirsty.

Austin was watching me. "Let me pour some water into the bottle's lid for you."

"The lid is too small, I'm afraid. Can you just pour it into my beak?" Opening my beak as wide as I could, I put my head back. Austin tried to pour carefully, but the water spilled over the sides of my beak before I could swallow. I shook the water off my feathers. "I'll fly on ahead and get some water from the pan in the ranger's hut."

"It will take us about twenty more minutes to get back," said Austin. "The panda is going to be really happy. I hope she's able to eat these shoots."

Megan came to the back of the line and walked next to us. "We were worried when you flew away, Luke. Maddie was afraid a Komodo might have gotten you." The pink shell glowed from her necklace. I was glad to see it was still working, even though I didn't think we needed it anymore. I'd already found the medicine woman and the pink Komodo. Now we just had to protect Roux and her eggs from Dunn Nikowski.

Chapter Ten—Outnumbered

"Don't give her too much at first," said Jake. "Her stomach might not accept it. That's right, isn't it, Luke?" His face was anxious as he waited for my approval.

"That's right." I nodded and smiled. It was the first time Jake had ever asked my opinion on anything. Was this the same kid who had pinched me until I was black and blue while we were at camp together?

Megan and Austin gently placed strands of bamboo near the panda. She promptly picked them up and stuffed them in her mouth. Then she pointed at the pile in their arms and squeaked at them. The panda's squeak sounded like someone had stepped on a baby toy.

We'd brought her outside to sit under a tree while we fed her. She hadn't had anything to eat in the three days we were on the boat and probably three or four more since they'd captured her in China. Giving her a lot all at once might make her sick. Or give her diarrhea. I didn't want her vomiting or pooping inside the Rangers' Station. After a half hour of feeding tasty bamboo twigs to the panda, I left her in Jake's care and took Megan and Austin aside.

"We have to go back and look for the cave. We don't have much time. If Dunn finds it first, he'll catch the Komodo and take off with it."

"How could he do that?" asked Megan. "How would he get the Komodo off the island?"

"He could put it on a boat at night, when everyone is asleep. A boat could come into a cove where no one goes." My feathers fluttered. I tried to keep the trembling out of my voice. "I heard him making arrangements with the captain of the boat that rescued the group in the lifeboat. He's supposed to come back tomorrow and get them."

Austin nodded. "That means he'll try to catch the Komodo today."

"Or tonight," added Megan.

"I think we should go now, while it's still light," I said firmly. "We need to find the cave the Elder described to us. After we find the pink Komodo, we have to protect it." I didn't tell them why.

Both of them were staring at me. Austin's brow was wrinkled as though he was thinking. Megan let out a long breath and sighed. "What do we need to take with us? We might be out all night."

"We need something to catch the Komodo with," said Austin. "Then we need food, water, a compass, matches, and maybe a map of the island."

We didn't need a compass or a map. I knew exactly where to go. I'd promised not to tell anyone I had found the cave; but I hadn't promised not to return.

"There's something else," said Megan. "The Komodos up there are wild. How can we defend ourselves if they attack?"

I laughed. "We can morph if we have to, and supersize. We'll have to be careful not to kill any of them. That's what caused all the trouble for Dunn and Gramps, and they're already endangered."

"We have to leave some kind of message for our folks," said Austin. "They'll be worried enough when we don't show up for dinner. We have to reassure them that we're okay, or they'll be out all night looking for us."

I agreed. "Is there a pencil and paper anywhere? We'll tell them we're looking for the cave the Elder told us about."

The only paper was in the bathroom. Megan pulled off five sheets of toilet tissue. She found a stub of a pencil in the drawer with the plastic eating utensils. Austin wrote the note, writing carefully so he wouldn't tear the paper. He left it on the table, weighing it down with a box of crackers. Then Megan and Austin filled their cloth bags with things we thought we would need, dividing them up. I couldn't help at all, so Austin took more than his share of the weight. He coiled the rope he'd bought from the captain of the fishing boat that rescued us and put his head and one arm through so he could carry it across his body. Megan took an extra bottle of water and a cup for me to use. When everything was packed, we set out to find the pink Komodo.

The mid-afternoon sun was still high, and the heat was stifling. I flew ahead as Austin and Megan followed me. They walked single file on a well-worn path that led up hill toward the edge of the mountains.

This is it, I thought. The curse on us had emerged eleven months ago, during that awful storm at the zoo. Now we were going to end it. It seemed like there should be a parade or trumpets blowing as we set off. Instead we were sneaking out of the village, trying to avoid Gramps, our parents, and Dunn Nikowski. I was flying low in the form of an eagle, watching my brother and my friend carry all the equipment as they trudged up the hill.

"It's too bad we couldn't trust Jake," said Austin. "We could probably have used his help."

I glanced back at him. "For what?"

"Catching the Komodo," said Austin. "We aren't sure how that's going to go yet."

I knew he was worried because I couldn't really help him if we ended up roping the Komodo. Austin was strong, but could he hold onto a bucking, two- or three-hundred-pound Komodo dragon all by himself? Having Jake along would give us another strong person to help. Of course I had to pretend that we still needed to catch the pink Komodo and bring her to the medicine woman, when all we really needed to do was make sure Roux's eggs hatched safely and that Dunn couldn't get near her or her babies.

"We have the shell necklace," I reminded Austin. "The Elder said we had what we needed to catch her."

As the path curved upward, the trail got steeper. Rocky outcrops jutted up between tufts of ragged grass. I flew back and forth, keeping an eye out for Komodos that could spring out from their hiding place and attack one of us.

After walking for about twenty minutes, Megan and Austin were soaked with sweat. We stopped to drink some water. I was pecking away at my cup when a faint sound of voices rang up over the hills. I signaled Megan and Austin to stay quiet. Then I flew to the top of a nearby tree to have a look. About a mile away, a group of men were on their way up the hill. I recognized some of them. They were Dunn Nikowski,

Captain Morrison, and another crew member. Two men from the village came behind them, pulling a large cart. On the cart was the big empty crate the men had been working on that morning. Behind the cart walked Mr. Burnell, the cook. The myna was perched on his shoulder.

Though I was in the form of an eagle, I had the Komodo's ability to hear. Dunn's voice was very clear. He was telling the men that the Komodo they wanted was no ordinary specimen. They were to catch a pink one. The men pulling the cart dropped their ropes. Then I heard some yelling. The men from the village were shaking their heads and walking away. It seemed they didn't want to help catch a pink dragon. Dunn yelled something about money, but the men kept walking. Finally Dunn and the cook picked up the ropes.

"What's going on?" whispered Austin.

I returned to where they were hiding and perched on the ground next to Megan. I told them what I'd heard.

"Serves them right," said Megan.

I flew back to the top of the tree. Now Mr. Burnell and Dunn were pulling the cart. They were heading in the direction of the fork. If they went right, they'd go down the hill toward the other side of the island. If they went to the left, they'd be heading toward us.

"Let's get out of here," I said. "If they get any closer, they'll see us." I flew in another direction, heading for the cave. It wasn't far. I thought we could get to it before Dunn's party could see us.

The rocky outcrops got bigger, and soon we were in the area where the grass touched the stone of the mountain. I flew along next to the mountain as I had that morning, watching for the entrance to the cave where I'd found Mairghread and

Roux. My heart pounded beneath my chest feathers. We were close to accomplishing what we'd come here to do.

Then I saw it. A flat rock about four feet high and three feet wide, propped against the side of the mountain. The "hole in the Whole" totem was cut into the mountain near it. Behind the flat rock was the opening into the cave.

"Here it is!" I cried. Austin and Megan came running. We entered together, with me in the lead. I squinted, trying to see more clearly. Any second now they would see what we had come across the world to find. First they would see the medicine woman. Mairghread would strike a match and reveal the pink Komodo. I couldn't wait to see their faces and hear them shout with joy. This was the moment. Checking to make sure they were behind me, I flew deeper into the cave and landed.

Everything was dark, as it had been when I entered that morning. I turned my head right and left, searching for the medicine woman and Roux. There were no shadows here, no shape of a woman sitting on a rock ledge. The cave was completely empty.

The medicine woman and a huge pink Komodo had been here just a few hours ago. Where had they gone? Where was the stream of water that flowed down the rock? Where was the pool of sweet, cold water? I flew frantically from one end of the cave to the other.

"I know this is the right place," I said, landing again.

"How do you know? There are probably a lot of caves," said Austin.

"The totem is outside," said Megan. "I saw it."

Austin turned on his flashlight and directed it around the cave. There seemed to be nothing but gray rock on the floor. Then he swept it across the back wall of the cave. "Man!

Look at this!" he exclaimed. Megan gasped. I felt weak with relief. I wasn't crazy.

It was all there. The paintings on the back wall of the cave glowed with color as Austin passed the circle of his light upon them. There were the gray Komodos and the wild pigs. There were the men returning from the hunt, and the mothers with their babies on their backs. People sat around an orange and yellow fire. I stayed quiet as Austin and Megan moved along the wall, looking at the figures. They stopped suddenly where the paintings ended. Megan uttered a cry of surprise.

"Gramps," said Austin. He pointed to a figure with a white navy cap on its head. "There's a gun in his hand."

Megan waved for me to come closer. "There's Dunn. His leg is bleeding. And there's the pink Komodo. It looks dead. Luke, look at these paintings. And look here, at this painting of Gramps and Dunn Nikowski. It shows who killed the pink Komodo! This is awful!"

I moved up next to them. I had to pretend that I'd never seen all this before. Had I missed anything? Were there symbols or pictures that would lead us to another place where Mairghread and Roux might hide?

Austin sighed. "It's as if the story ended with Gramps and Dunn."

I closed my beak hard to keep from telling them what Mairghread had told me. Nothing more had been painted since that awful day. Everything had changed for the islanders, and now no one seemed to have the heart to paint.

"We have to find the pink Komodo," said Megan. "We must keep looking."

"There's something over here," said Austin. "It's an entrance to another cave." He slid through to the other side. Megan and I followed. Austin had focused his light on something in the corner.

"What is it?" asked Megan.

"Eggs." Austin focused his light on them so we could see. They're big—six or seven inches long." I watched, happy that he'd found them. That was one secret I no longer had to keep.

"We have to keep them safe," I said. "These are the pink Komodo's eggs."

"How do you know?" Austin reached out to touch one.

"This is a special place," I answered. "The paintings show that."

Megan was staring at me, an odd expression on her face. "Are you sure you've told us everything?" she asked.

There was nothing more I could tell them. They might not believe me anyway. There was no sign that Mairghread and the pink Komodo had been here. If it hadn't been for the cave paintings, I might not have believed it myself.

"I've told you everything I can," I said. "Please, let's just think a minute. How can we keep these eggs safe?"

"They're safe as long as no one finds the cave," said Austin. "It's pretty well hidden."

"I wonder where the pink Komodo is." I glanced around, looking for tracks in the dust on the cave floor. Nothing. There were no shoeprints except ours. Then I remembered that she'd given me a drink of sweet, cold water. I hurried toward the place where the little pool had been. There was a shallow depression in the floor at the back of the cave. Water had trickled down the wall into a little pool, right in this spot. It relieved my thirst so completely that it filled me with hope. I stared at the dry shallow bowl in the cave floor. Megan and Austin came to my side.

"That's interesting," said Austin. "Something eroded that space from the rock." He knelt, feeling the bottom and sides of the circular depression. "Dry as a bone." His eyes went to the vertical ridge that traveled the length of the cave ceiling and disappeared somewhere over our heads. "My guess is the water trickled down this ridge from an opening in the rock overhead somewhere. It must have been that way for hundreds of years to hollow this out."

Megan pointed to a place on the barely visible drawings on the cave wall. I moved nearer, and the pink light from the shell necklace began to glow. It lit up the section of the wall nearest to us.

"There!" cried Megan. "Look!" A picture of water, streaming to a pool below, had been painted on the rock. Something was drinking at the pool. As Megan moved sideways, a creature became visible, the snout bent toward the water. Its long, faintly pink body was poised on four stubby legs. The tail stretched past roughly drawn figures that knelt nearby, their hands holding bowls. Their heads were bowed, as though they were offering something to the dragon. Megan drew in her breath.

"We've found the sacred cave," whispered Austin. I stayed close to Megan as she moved so the pink shell would stay lit.

"It must have been here, and not too long ago," said Austin. "The eggs were clean. No dirt or dust or anything to suggest they'd been here for a while."

"Do you think the babies are alive? In the eggs, I mean." Megan eyed me anxiously.

"Sure." I said. But I was thinking about something else. "I think we should go. Dunn and his men were heading for the other side of the island. Maybe they've spotted the pink Komodo over there."

We headed out and started down the hill. We'd gone about fifty yards when I heard a strange sound. It was low, as though something was chewing. Careless, like an animal. Layered, like several animals. Gobbling. Crunching. Ripping. Growling. Snapping. Gulping.

Austin stopped walking, his head down as though he was listening. "What is that?" he asked softly.

"What?" Megan frowned. "I can't hear anything."

Both Austin and Megan knew I could sense feelings and communication from other animals. For reptiles, I could only get vague sensations. I was getting some of those now. Hunger. Wanting more. Mindless tearing at the prey. Sensations of pressure from all sides. The feelings swamped me as though I was drowning. Komodo dragons—I couldn't be sure how many—were up ahead.

Austin and Megan were watching my face.

"How many?" asked Austin. His hand was on his pocket. I wasn't sure what he was reaching for, but I hoped it was a weapon. Goosebumps prickled under my feathers.

"Between ten and twenty," I said, trying not to sound alarmed. It was probably closer to twenty.

"How far?" Megan's voice trembled.

"Less than half a mile," I said. "Maybe closer."

Megan's eyes were wide with fear. "Should we hide?"

"Let's make sure we're downwind," said Austin. He pointed to a chunk of rock formation to the north of us. "We can climb up on those rocks and into that tree." He pointed toward a tall tree about twenty yards away, back toward the cave.

"Good idea. Grab your stuff, Megan." I wished I could take some of it from their shoulders. Austin hoisted the two cloth bags and followed me. I flew low, staying in front of them.

"What if it's occupied?" Megan sounded breathless. I knew it was from fear, not running.

"We'll find another tree," I answered. "Hurry."

Austin went up first, examining the branches cautiously as he climbed. Extending a hand down to Megan, he hauled her up onto the limb beside him. I flew past her and landed about twenty feet above their heads. Peering out over the hilly grass, I narrowed my eyes until I saw an undulating gray mound—a moving hill. Only it wasn't a hill. It was a huge pile of heaving, shifting, scaly gray bodies. Komodos! Tails flapped and torsos twisted as they burrowed downward toward some kind of carcass. Hooved legs stood straight up in the air, stiff and dead, moving awkwardly as the Komodos feasted around them. A ribcage of something that was once pretty big—water buffalo maybe—had collapsed to one side.

"How many?" asked Austin.

"About twenty, I think. They're scrambling all over each other." I tried to keep the fear out of my voice.

Megan gasped, then covered her mouth with her hand. None of us moved, or even breathed. If they caught wind of us, we were done for. Austin was scanning everything, looking for an escape route. There was no way we could defend ourselves from so many Komodos, absorbed in their goal of devouring whatever food they could find.

I forced myself to turn and meet their eyes. Megan's were wide and terrified, Austin's reluctant.

"It's the only way," he breathed. I nodded. We had no

choice. If we didn't morph, we wouldn't be able to defend our-selves.

The sound of a shot echoed in the distance. A red flare soared into the air. The gobbling noises stopped abruptly. Twenty snouts shot upwards, snapping to the left like marines on parade. The Komodos weren't looking at the flare. They had been distracted from the carcass long enough to catch our scent. Twenty pairs of beady black eyes stared in our direc-tion, eager for a better feast. The gray mountain of scales shifted and fell apart. Long gray bodies trotted toward us.

"Get moving," I cried. "Get higher!"

"Let's not!" Austin pointed upwards. Five green and yel-low striped snouts and five pairs of beady little eyes stared down at us from the limb overhead. Five venomous little mouths opened, showing dagger sharp teeth. In my eagerness to watch the mound of adult Komodos, I'd flown right past these dangerous babies. The Komodos had us surrounded.

Austin climbed down so he was next to Megan. His wristband pressed against hers as he clasped her hand.

A pink light began to glow around us.

"Put it out!" whispered Austin, his tone harsh with panic. The pink light flickered on and off, like a lighthouse.

"I'm not touching it!" My voice was frantic too. I edged along a limb away from Megan, making sure.

The glow enlarged, taking in the earth around us, reveal-ing grass and rocks and skittering insects. A bird shrieked and flew away. I wanted to follow it. Could I? Yes! That was it. I could grow to the size of my bedroom and carry one friend with each talon.

A bell tinkled, small and sweet. The sound came, low at first, as if floating over the floor of the earth and around us. I felt myself being grabbed on both sides—Megan's hand on one wing and Austin's painful grip on the other. The tinkling bell grew louder. A pink bubble grew up from the bottom of the tree, surrounding us. Just ahead, there was movement from the direction of the mountain. An enormous pink head turned in our direction, followed by a flurry of glowing scales and pink-tinged legs and claws.

"I'm not getting eaten," whispered Megan. "I don't care if this thing is pink or chartreuse green. I'm out of here!"

She didn't move. None of us could move. We were paralyzed within the translucent pink bubble, the light still blinking and singing from the shell on Megan's necklace.

The pink Komodo moved ahead as if to speak to the twenty or so drooling lizards. Step by step, her enormous body pushing her feet deep into the ground, Roux flopped forward, her heavy belly dragging in the dirt. She showed no interest in us after that first glance.

"We're gonna need a bigger rope!" whispered Austin.

"You think?" I whispered back.

"Hush," whispered Megan.

"She knows we're here, Meg," said Austin.

"They all know we're here," I grumbled.

The pink Komodo continued her slow walk down the hill. As she moved, the pink bubble melted away. The gray Komodos fell into line behind her.

"She's getting away," cried Megan. "What can we do?"

"I don't know," I answered. "The other Komodos are with her."

Austin climbed down and peered around the tree. He looked back at us, smiling. "They're walking down the hill, quiet as can be. It's like they're sleep-walking."

Megan climbed down, and I perched higher up in the tree, staying well away from the venomous babies. The Komodos continued down the hill. They walked slowly, one foot after the other, marching together like a band. Their snouts were pointed straight ahead. They didn't flick their tongues or look from right to left or up or down. They stepped together like zombies on parade, their legs stiff as Frankenstein's. When they turned down the hill toward the ocean, I flew down and landed next to Austin and Megan.

"That was close," I said.

"I was so scared," said Megan. "I'm still shaking."

"Me too," said Austin. "Are you okay, Luke?"

I nodded. "My heart was pounding so hard I thought you guys could hear it."

"What caused the tinkling bells?" asked Austin. "Did the sound come from the shell?"

Megan took the shell pendant gently in her hand. "I think so. It was as if the sound called to the pink Komodo."

"The Elder said we had what we needed to find the pink Komodo," I added. "He also said we had what we needed to protect ourselves. Did he mean the shell necklace?"

"I think he meant our wristbands," said Megan. "The bell sound started when my wristband touched Austin's. "Then the pink bubble floated up the hill and paralyzed us."

"It seemed like the pink Komodo was protecting us," said Austin. "She led the Komodos away."

"I think that's the most scared I've ever been," said Megan. "No, I take that back. The most scared I've ever been is when I fell from the water tower at the zoo."

"Don't remind me," I said. "That was terrifying."

"You saved my life." Megan's voice was soft.

"You saved mine, too," said Austin. "I think you saved all of us that day at the zoo."

"All but Megan," I said. "She saved me by biting Dunn so I could go through the twirling tunnel. Then she was left behind." I winced, just thinking about that terrible time when we were first changed into animals. I'd learned a lot from that experience. So had Austin. We were completely different people now.

"You saved me later, when you came back," said Megan. "That's when I fell from the water tower."

Austin took a deep breath. "We've lived through some tough times this past year. I'm glad this will soon be over and we can get out of this place."

"It's not over yet," I reminded them. "We still have to protect the pink Komodo and her eggs. We have to keep them safe from Dunn Nikowski."

Chapter Eleven—What is in the One is in the Whole

It was getting dark. We went back to the cave to rest.

"Let's have some water and a snack," said Austin. He reached into his pocket and brought out two Snickers bars.

I gaped at him. "Where'd you get those?" There weren't any candy stores on Komodo Island. He kept producing Snickers bars like a magician.

"I got these two from another guy on the fishing boat," said Austin. "I gave him a U.S. dollar." He broke each candy bar into three pieces. He handed two pieces to Megan and dropped one into my beak. It was hard to chew and not much fun. I gulped it down.

"Our folks know we're out here somewhere," said Megan. She unscrewed the cap on her water bottle, gulped some down, and handed it to Austin. "They must have shot off the flare we saw. How can we tell them where we are?"

"I'm afraid they'll think we were under that pile of Komodos," I said. I perched next to Austin. "No phones, no internet, no walkie-talkies. What were we thinking?"

We'd been stupid to come out here on our own with no

way of communicating. We had to let our folks know where we were and that we were safe. Otherwise they might try to come up here after us. Those Komodos would be back sooner or later. Even with the four adults in our party, the Komodos outnumbered us two or three to one.

"I could fly back and get help, but I don't want to leave you guys here alone. What if the Komodos came back? Even if both of you supersized, you wouldn't be able to fight off twenty of them." Megan shivered. Austin nodded. He knew I was right.

"Let's think about this," said Austin. "You sensed the thoughts of the wolves at the zoo, and then the cougar at camp. You heard Megan when she was an upside-down turtle."

Megan shuddered. "Don't remind me."

I closed my eyes. If only I could reach Gramps and Mom the way I communicated with the animals. Then I remembered something. "Meg, you were able to wake me with your thoughts when I was sound asleep. Our folks will be wide awake and looking for us."

"You contacted us when we weren't in animal form, right?" Austin sat up a little straighter. "They've all morphed, even Aunt Jo. Maybe you can reach them with your thoughts the same way you reached us."

"They're farther away than the other animals were," I said. "But it's worth a try."

"Maybe if we did it together, we could reach them," said Megan. Her smile lit up her face. "Let's try it. Luke, tell us what to say in our thoughts."

"Close your eyes," I instructed. "Try to quiet your mind. Take a deep breath. Now another. In through your nose, out through your mouth." Austin and Megan both sat cross-legged with their eyes closed. They both looked calm, so I continued my instructions. "Imagine everyone together, trying to decide what to do. Now send this in your thoughts.

Hello everyone. We're in a cave at the top of the hill where the grass meets the mountain. Turn right at the bamboo forest and head north about a mile. Be careful. Large pack of Komodos were in front of the cave, but they've gone down the hill some-where. Make sure you can defend yourselves. We're safe inside the cave."

We repeated it again, all of us concentrating on sending the same message. Then each of us sent it alone, hoping that our specific relatives would pick it up.

A noise made me open my eyes. Austin and Megan's eyes were open too. I gave them the "stay quiet" signal. I peeked outside. There were no Komodos in sight. No people, either. I went back to perch next to Austin. He and Megan were talking about catching the pink Komodo.

"We'll find her again. The Elder said the bracelets would help us." Megan turned the bracelet on her wrist and touched the little heart. I peered at it.

"There's the tiny circle," I said, pointing to it on the heart. "The heart itself must be the larger Whole." I traced a circle in the air with the tips of my wings. The medicine wom-an had explained that we were all connected. The Whole meant our world, our energy, linked together with the energy of all living things on our earth. And perhaps beyond. I'd have to ask Gramps about that.

"I wonder what else this thing can do," said Austin. He turned the bracelet on his wrist.

"I'm tired," said Megan. "Let's rest for a bit before we go

back outside. At least it's cool in here."

She closed her eyes and so did Austin. I blinked, trying to stay awake. But I hadn't slept well the night before. I decided to close my eyes for a few minutes.

It wasn't very long before we heard some kind of commotion going on outside.

"Stay put. I'll have a look." Austin shoved himself to his feet and slid through to the outer cave. A few minutes later we heard him give a long, exaggerated sigh. "We got through to them. The cavalry is coming to our rescue."

I flew to his side with Megan close behind me. We peered out the cave's opening. Megan laughed. It looked more like the circus was coming to our rescue. Led by a cougar, several animals were galloping up the hill. A wolverine, a silverback gorilla, a wolf, and a wild boar all hurried in our direction.

The pack of carnivores slowed to a stop. They seemed to be looking around, trying to find the cave.

I rose into the air, flapping my wings. "We're here, in the cave. We're all fine," I called.

The cougar rolled on the ground, and Mom stood up. The wolverine had morphed back too. Gramps sat down with his back against the cave, panting. "I'm getting too old for this."

"I told you not to come," said Mr. Gifford. "We could have handled it."

"Like I was going to let the rest of you face an army of Komodos," said Gramps.

Aunt Jo, no longer a wolf, and Mr. Gifford, morphing back from the gorilla, followed Mom into the cave. Jake, who'd morphed back from his wild boar form, stopped to grin at me.

"How's the panda getting along?" I asked.

His smile grew wider. "Okay. I let her eat for a while, then I took her for a little walk. I didn't want to have to clean up a mess in the bunk area when we got back."

I couldn't believe that Jake was taking over pooper-scooper duties. He really cared about that panda. Maybe all he needed to become a real human being was a pet. I'd have to suggest that to Aunt Jo.

I touched him with the tip of my right wing. "You do know you can't take the panda home with you, right?"

The smile faded and the corners of his mouth turned down. "I know. She needs to go home." He stared out into the distance for a few seconds. "How can we get her to China?"

"We haven't figured that out yet. We're hoping the ranger will help us. You can think about it and try to come up with some ideas. Austin, Megan, and I have something else to do."

A strange expression crossed his face. He knew we were after the pink Komodo. His grandfather wanted it too. Who would Jake help? Us or his grandfather? He had a big decision to make. We would be doing the right thing by protecting the Komodo and seeing that Dunn didn't take it. Dunn's motives were money and power. Jake knew that, but it would be hard to go against his own grandfather.

Some good things had happened to Jake on this trip. When we were on the ship, his mom had told him the real story of why she had to leave him with his father. Then he found the panda and had risked his life to help me rescue it when the ship was sinking. The more he took care of the panda, the more it trusted him. That was good for Jake. It was too bad the panda couldn't go to a good zoo like the one where we lived. Then Jake could visit her every week, if he wanted to.

Right now, Megan, Austin, and I had to think about finding the pink Komodo. We had to protect her and her eggs so this curse could be undone. Roux had just walked past the three of us and led about twenty gray Komodos down the hill. She must have gotten away from the medicine woman somehow. We needed to go after her now, before she got too far ahead of us. She'd gone in the same direction as Dunn and his men. I tried to tell the others this, but they wouldn't listen.

Mom passed around bottles of water and snack bars. Aunt Jo unloaded sandwiches and chips. I tried to tell them we didn't have time to eat, but Mom insisted. She said it would help us keep our brains sharp so we could think and plan. So we all sat down on a blanket in front of the cave and shared the food.

"How did you find us?" I asked, as Mom passed the chips. They all stopped what they were doing and looked at each other. They seemed unsure about answering the question. Finally Gramps spoke up.

"We all heard your message," said Gramps. "At first I thought I was the only one who heard it. I thought it could be my imagination. So I mentioned it to your mom."

"I told him I'd heard it too," said Mom. "I heard the exact same words he did, and at the same time."

"Jo told me she had a hunch where Megan might be," said Mr. Gifford. "She said she'd received a message. I'd gotten one also, so we compared them."

"It didn't take us long to figure out that you'd sent the message deliberately," said Gramps. "We were amazed that you could do it. But there was no other explanation."

"I don't get it," said Jake. He pointed to me and Austin. "How could you guys send a mental message to my mom and the others? It's spooky."

"Not really," said Gramps. "There are lots of examples of people knowing that someone they love is in trouble. Some people believe all thoughts are telepathic if you want them to be."

Jake scrunched up his forehead. "What does that mean?"

"That means the person you are thinking about knows you are thinking about them. Then they call you and you think it's a coincidence. But it isn't. Your thought waves reached them somehow," explained Gramps.

"The Elder said something like that," I added. Everyone looked toward me, waiting. "He said that when Dunn poked that Komodo all those years ago, it made a tear in the Whole, or the great oneness that we all share." I spread my wings and tried to make a big circle on the word "oneness."

"It made a hole in the Whole," said Megan. She and Austin both made a large circle with their arms as Megan spoke the word "Whole." I spread my wings again, drawing a circle in the air—as if the three of us were putting on a little show. But we weren't. Though we didn't completely understand the words, we were all convinced that what the Elder said was true. The medicine woman had said those same words to me that morning. I wished so much that I could tell everyone I'd seen her, but I kept my promise and shut my beak.

The adults glanced from one of us to the other. Aunt Jo tilted her head and pursed her lips. Mr. Gifford's eyebrows squished together. Mom nodded slowly, her eyes intent on me. Jake puffed air into his cheeks and blew it out again. Gramps smiled. Professor Kenwood had probably been teaching the "oneness" idea in his classes all along.

I pecked at my sandwich, then my water. Nothing tasted

good. I didn't want to eat anyway. We had to find Roux and her eggs and make sure they were okay. The eggs had been in the inner cave before we left. They were probably still safe there unless someone in Dunn's party had found them. The pink Komodo had gone the same direction Dunn had gone, and that worried me. What about the twenty Komodos that marched, zombielike, down the hill, following Roux? Wherever they went, I hoped they'd stay there until we were far from Komodo Island.

"We have to get going," I said, flapping my wings. "We don't have time to sit around here eating and talking. Every minute, Dunn could be getting closer to the pink Komodo."

Gramps frowned. Mom and Aunt Jo looked at each other and then at me. I told them we'd seen Dunn and several men head for the ocean a few hours earlier. The Komodos had gone toward the ocean too.

"If they take that pink Komodo away, or kill her, we'll never be able to undo the curse!" I couldn't keep the catch out of my voice, and my tone was sharp. Just thinking about being an eagle forever made me feel desperate. If we didn't undo this curse, I'd never graduate from high school or go to college. Eagles didn't have many taste buds, so I wouldn't be able to enjoy ice cream or pancakes or blueberry muffins. I'd be eating raw fish and sleeping standing up for the rest of my life. Tears overflowed my eyes. I couldn't wipe them away, so I blinked to get rid of them.

Gramps put his arm around the top of my eagle body and hugged me. "We'll fix this, Luke. I promise you. We'll fix it."

The medicine woman had promised me that too. But here I was, still an eagle. Where was the medicine woman now? I gave myself a shake and flapped my wings. This was no time to sit around feeling sorry for myself. I had work to do.

"Okay," I said. "Dunn will need a ship to take the Komodo away if he captures it. It could be here already. So we'll head toward the water. When we get to the bamboo trees, everyone needs to stay back where they can't be seen. I'll fly ahead and see where they are and what they're doing. Then we'll figure out how to stop them."

I glanced at the sky. The moon was high above us. It would give us enough light to see where we were going. All of the adults had one of the cloth bags Austin had purchased from a woman in the village. Gramps took a set of walkie-talkies from his bag and gave one of them to Austin. Mr. Gifford didn't have a flashlight, but Austin had two. He handed one to Mr. Gifford. Aunt Jo packed up the rest of the sandwiches and the water bottles. She and Mom put the food and water in their bags. Soon we were on our way.

We were nearing the bamboo forest when we saw Katerie hurrying along the path. "I'm going with you," she called. "I feel my mother calling me. I think she might be in trouble." That didn't sound good. If the medicine woman was in trouble, Roux was in trouble as well.

Following my plan, everyone stayed back in the trees while I soared ahead to see if I could spot Dunn and his party. I saw lights in the distance, about two miles away. Some of the men were on a narrow beach between the sea and a grassy hill that ran along the mountainside. A large fishing boat was anchored off shore. It was the same fishing boat that had picked up the crew of the lifeboat and their passengers. Mr. Brownlee had returned for them after all.

I landed in a tree and perched on a high limb, then focused in on them. The crate was there, sitting at a slant of grassy hill that ran along the mountainside. It was about a hundred yards up the hill from the beach. The hinged door on one end of the crate was open, just a few feet from a dark opening into the mountain. It had to be another cave. Perhaps Dunn had already found Roux.

What I saw next made my heart sink. A woman with long white hair was tied to a tree near the beach. She wore a long white top and a long skirt, and her hands were tied in front of her. How could Dunn treat an elderly woman that way? Katerie was right. Her mother was in trouble.

Dunn tied a big chunk of raw meat to the end of a rope. Standing in front of the crate's open door, he threw the meat forward. It disappeared into the mountain. When he dragged the rope out again, the meat was gone.

He tied another piece of meat to the end of the rope and tossed it again, letting the meat land just outside the cave. A scaly pink leg reached out and tried to grab the meat. My heart started to pound. Roux was there, only a few feet from them!

Dunn shortened the rope and tried to pull the meat backwards. He tugged at the rope, but it seemed to be stuck on something. Then Dunn skidded forward toward the cave as if he were the one being reeled in. He dropped the rope and stepped quickly away. The medicine woman laughed. Dunn spun on her, a scowl on his face. "Shut up!" he yelled. The pink Komodo obviously wasn't cooperating, and neither was Mairghread. I hoped one of them would bite him.

I flew back to the bamboo forest, staying low so no one would see me. Everyone was sitting on the ground, waiting for me. I landed next to Austin and folded in my wings.

"Did you see them?" asked Austin.

"Yes," I said. I told them what I'd seen. "The pink Komodo is still in the cave. We have to make sure Dunn doesn't get her."

"It's illegal to take Komodos from the island," said Gramps. "I'm going to call the rangers and ask them to call the police."

I controlled an impulse to squawk at him. Austin, Megan, and I were going to have to use our animal forms to free the pink Komodo. What were the police going to think when they arrived and saw a Komodo or a grizzly bear fighting with the crew of a fishing boat and a man with two artificial legs?

I took a deep breath. "It will take them a while to get here, Gramps. The pink Komodo and the medicine woman could be dead by then. We have to act now."

Chapter Twelve—Saving Roux

"You have to decide whose side you're on, Jake. If you're going to stand with your grandfather, you'd better go down there now."

Jake raised his eyes to mine. Then he looked at Gramps, who'd stood up for him that morning. His eyes went to his mother. She clasped his arm and smiled. He glanced at Megan, who gave him a "thumbs up," and then at his Uncle Roy, who simply nodded. Last, his eyes were on mine again. "I'm with you," he said. His voice was firm.

Spreading my wings a little, I turned back to the group. "Austin, Megan, and I will take care of Dunn. The rest of you will watch Dunn's men. If they try to help Dunn or capture the pink Komodo, you'll have to stop them. Use your animal forms if necessary."

Austin had carried the rope he'd bought from the fisherman in his bag. He handed it to Mom. "I might need this," he said. "Keep it handy so you can toss it to me."

"Let me go in instead of Megan," said Jake. "I'm stronger."

I shook my head. "She's faster and deadlier, Jake. She could kill you in a couple of seconds. You need to help the others. Keep an eye on the cook, Burnell."

Jake nodded his agreement.

Each of us was limited to three animals. Megan could be a death adder, a giant bullfrog, or a giant turtle. Austin's forms were the grizzly bear, elephant, and dolphin. I'd turned into a Komodo dragon, a hippo, and an eagle. Each form gave us both abilities and limitations. We'd have to use the one most likely to defeat whatever form Dunn chose—and he seemed to have more than three. At the zoo, Dunn had morphed into a gigantic cobra, a huge hyena, and the monstrous crocodile. He'd supersized all those animals. Dunn had also turned up on the ship in the form of a rat. Even the rat would be dangerous if it was ten feet long.

We set out again, keeping the flashlights off. I led them to the tree I'd perched in before, to take one more look. Dunn was still trying to lure Roux out with chunks of meat. His men gathered around him, watching. Why didn't they just go into the cave and capture the pink Komodo? The medicine woman couldn't prevent them; she was tied to a tree near the cave. Her hands were tied together and her head and shoulders slumped forward. She wouldn't be able to breathe very well like that. I sent her a mental message that help was on the way. She lifted her head, but didn't look in our direction. If she had, she could have alerted Dunn that we were there.

Dunn tossed the meat again, letting it drop just outside the cave. After a brief pause, a huge pink snout came out of the cave and sniffed at it. Roux grabbed the meat and backed into the cave again. I tried not to laugh out loud.

Dunn's plan wasn't working. What else would he do? A

large fishing net—the kind they drag through the water to catch lots of fish—was piled to one side of the crate. They could throw that over the Komodo, if they could get her to come out. I also noticed something black in the grass next to it, along with a package of tubes with wicks. I focused in on the tubes, examining them closely. Those were sticks of dynamite!

I flew back to the group and landed on the ground.

"What's wrong?" whispered Austin.

"They have dynamite," I whispered back. "We have to protect Roux. I'm going to get rid of it. Don't come down to the beach until I've dropped it in the ocean."

"You won't have much time," warned Austin. "Maybe only ten seconds after he lights them."

I nodded. "Start down the hill when I grab it." Everyone was watching me. Gramps had his hand on Mom's arm, as if to keep her from running after me. "I'll be okay," I said, trying to reassure her.

Rising quietly into the air, I glided above the crate. Dunn was holding the batch of dynamite sticks in one hand and a cigarette lighter in the other. He flicked the lighter and touched a small flame to the wick of one of the sticks of dynamite. It caught. The wick flickered and started to burn.

I dove so fast he didn't see me coming. Talons down, I yanked the dynamite tubes from Dunn's hand, then sped up into the sky at seventy miles an hour. The flame flashed and then died, extinguished by the rush of air created by my speed. Up, up, up into the sky I went, gripping Dunn's dynamite pack with my talons. I circled for a few seconds, then sped downward, dropping the explosives into the water, far from the shore and well away from the reef and the ship.

Dunn ran to the edge of the beach, gesturing and shouting at me. His men watched, open-mouthed. None of them paid any attention to the six people who were sneaking down the hill. They moved onto the beach just as I neared the shore, spreading out near Dunn's men.

Dunn's face was red and angry. He picked up a wooden slat and smacked my leg with it as I tried to land, knocking me through the air. I hit the dirt several feet from him. Fiery pain shot through my body, but I stayed upright. Coming up behind him, Austin grabbed the slat away from him and threw it into the ocean. Dunn scooped something black out of the grass. It was about two feet long, with two short, metal rods on the end. It was a cattle prod, like the one he'd had in the zoo! Dunn jabbed Austin in the belly with it. Austin shrieked and doubled over.

Megan turned death adder as I went Komodo. We both morphed so fast we nearly collided as we attacked Dunn. Both of us got a mouthful of the metal leg. Megan struck again, biting him three times on the arm before he noticed her. Dunn rolled in the dirt, kicking up yards of dust. When the dust settled, a crocodile swished its long tail. Opening its wide jaws, it snapped at us. Dunn's decision to go croc was smart. It would take longer for the death adder's venom to poison a crocodile, if it had any effect at all.

Still in my Komodo form, I moved slowly around the croc, staying away from its snout and jagged teeth. It turned with me, making a sound like a swallowed roar. My right leg hurt, and I wasn't sure I could take the croc in Komodo form. If I supersized, I'd just have a bigger lame leg. I'd have to go hippo. A big hippo.

Behind us, more men came out of hiding. I counted at

least twelve, six on the boat and six gathering around us. Mr. Burnell was with them, Maggie the myna bird still clinging to his shoulder. "Dead by morning! Dead by morning!" she squawked.

The men moved closer. Most of them were carrying long sticks or big rocks. A van-sized cougar pounced out from behind a tree, followed by a wolf as big as a horse. The villagers took off, screaming as they ran up the hill and out of the fray. Five men were still on the beach with Dunn. From the corner of my eye, I saw a giant wolverine headed toward us, followed by a monster silverback gorilla.

Austin limped closer to me, holding his stomach. Megan coiled herself between us, ready to strike.

"Take them," shrieked Dunn. Three men surrounded me, holding the net. The man who had picked up the cattle prod jammed it into my belly, but it was too late. The tough hippo hide didn't even feel it. I opened my huge mouth and snapped my jaws down on the crocodile. All I got was a mouthful of air. A small rat ran across the beach.

A garage-sized bullfrog hopped after the rat, unrolling a long, sticky tongue. She slapped it against the rat, rolling it up like a bug. A second later the Megan-frog was holding a mouthful of fur. She spit it out like a hairball. The Dunn-hyena shot out in all directions, growing to the size of a jeep. It sprang at me, mouth open. A hairy fist the size of a small tire came down on its head, flattening it into a speckled, furry pancake. My brother had grown his bear form two-stories high. He scooped the hyena up and threw it into the ocean. A second later a bolt of electricity shot through me as one of Dunn's men hit me with the cattle prod. This time it hurt.

Growling, the cougar leapt between us. The man

dropped the cattle prod and ran. The angry Mom-cougar was faster. She pounced on the man and held him down with her paws. Aunt Jo, now a gigantic black wolf, loped along behind her, knocking down the cook. "Dead by morning! Dead by morning!" cried the myna bird. She flew away.

The wolf ran its tongue around its mouth. A drop of drool fell on the cook's face.

"Now what?" asked the Jo-wolf. She turned her pointed black snout toward the cougar, awaiting instructions. "Should we eat them?"

Mr. Burnell screamed from under her massive black paws.

"No," said my mother. "The meat wouldn't be good." The big cat turned its head toward the cave. "Uh oh," she growled.

I turned to check on Mairghread, just in time to see Jake, momentarily human, help Katerie untie her from the tree. He hurried both women along the beach, away from the cave. Behind them came shadowy movement.

Now we knew why Dunn and his men wouldn't go into the cave. Three gray Komodos peeked out of the opening, flicking their yellow forked tongues. They crept out, one at a time, sniffing the ground. The first one gulped a chunk of meat that lay on the ground. Two more Komodos crept out, hissing and flicking their tongues. They tore what was left of the meat from the first Komodo. I lost count as several more Komodos waddled out of the cave, so many that they jammed together in the opening. Growling, sniffing, and hissing, they moved toward us.

The cougar and the wolf padded next to us. I was still Komodo. Mr. Gifford was in silverback gorilla form, but gorillas aren't fighters. Austin had gone grizzly, but both of us were injured. Megan's forms wouldn't work with the Komodos. Snakes couldn't bite through their armor-like scales.

The Komodos thumped down the hill on their stubby bowed legs. Gramps, still a wolverine, and Mr. Gifford moved in next to us, so we faced outward as the Komodos circled. Five were well ahead of the others, then ten. Ten became fifteen, then all twenty gained speed as they charged down the hill.

"Supersize," I yelled. "As big as you can! Focus!" My body started to change, rippling up until I was three times bigger than the other Komodos. My right leg was still sore, but I could move it. Next to me, a twenty-foot-tall grizzly roared so loudly the nearest five Komodos jumped backwards. A two-ton bullfrog hopped up and down, croaking like cannon fire. Two of the Komodos backed away, but five more came closer.

"Megan!" I yelled. "Go turtle and pull in!"

The Mom-cougar and the Jo-wolf galloped around us, snarling at the Komodos. The Komodos snapped back at them. Mr. Gifford's silverback gorilla was now bigger than an elephant. He smacked one of the Komodos on top of the head with his gigantic fist. The Komodo flattened out and stayed down.

"Try not to kill them," I yelled.

"We can't reason with them, Luke!" shouted the cougar. "We don't have any choice!"

Shaking his tusked head, Jake reappeared as a wild boar, grown to the size of a hippo. The Komodos didn't advance on him, so he went after them, digging in his tusks and tossing first one, then another away from the group. The Gramps-wolverine was now twice the size of a lion. It snapped and bit, darting in and out wherever it looked like the Komodos were winning. With its razor-sharp claws, the giant wolverine had the best chance of piercing their scaly armor.

The Komodos attacked and retreated, jaws ready to inject venom into anything they could bite. They had us surrounded, two or three Komodos trying to take each of us down. A Komodo could take down a water buffalo, and they weren't afraid of any of us. To them, we were just a lively food supply. We could go bigger and kill them all, but their species was already endangered, and we didn't want to harm them.

"Jake!" I yelled. "Your mother needs help!" Two Komodos were snapping at the wolf's back leg. If a Komodo bit her, the venom would keep the blood from clotting. She would just keep bleeding. Everywhere I looked, my family was in danger of those venomous bites. We were losing this battle.

"Megan!" I shouted. "What did you do before? To make them go away?"

"Austin! Come here! Hurry!" called Megan. The grizzly moved towards her, followed by two Komodos.

"Keep them off us, Gramps," yelled Austin, kicking them away. "We have to go human for this."

The Gramps-wolverine bounded over. He sprang at one Komodo's back legs, raking them with razor-sharp claws. The Komodo twisted back, snapping with jagged teeth, catching nothing but a mouthful of air. The wolverine crouched, then pounced on the other Komodo, diving out of the way just in time. He sprang, pounced, and danced away, keeping three Komodos busy.

Within our dusty, shuffling circle, Austin and Megan turned human. Megan's shell necklace glowed pink, blinking and singing as the Komodos snarled and attacked.

"Quick, your wristband!" cried Megan.

Austin stretched to awkwardly press his wristband against hers while he kicked a snapping Komodo under the jaw. The tingle of tiny bells flowed out over the wild, chaotic scene, and everything went still.

Animals froze in mid-strike. Komodos' jaws stayed open, their claws poised in mid-air. A giant pink bubble floated down the hill and settled gently around us. No one moved. No one *could* move. We were frozen in place by the bubble, just as we had been before.

Something huge and pink drifted down the hill from the direction of the Komodos'cave, dragging its belly in the dust. An enormous pink head turned in our direction, followed by a flurry of glowing scales and rose-tinged legs and claws. Just as before, the pink Komodo stopped as though to speak to the giant lizards surrounding us. She turned, heading back up the hill. The Komodos fell into formation, stubby legs in sync and snouts pointed straight ahead. Stepping together like a marching band, they followed Roux back to the cave.

Then the pink bubble popped, and we unfroze to find the Dunn croc still with us, waiting just beyond the border of bubble-protection. Austin instantly threw the fishing net over its long body. The huge reptile's head came up as it snapped at the net. It rolled around, trying to throw the net off, but the more it moved, the more the net tangled around it.

The medicine woman appeared at our side, along with her daughter, Katerie. Mairghread raised her stick and clomped it down next to the crocodile's head. "Enough. If any of you morph again, you will stay that way."

All around me, animal forms dissolved into humans. Austin and Megan had already assumed their normal forms. The wolverine disappeared, and Gramps stood in its place.

The great tawny cougar shook its head and my mother returned. She put her hand on the wolf's head. It whined, moving about on its paws as if it didn't know what to do. I didn't know what to do either. I closed my eyes and tried to morph back to human. Nothing happened. When I opened my eyes, I was still covered with feathers. I still had wings instead of arms and talons instead of feet. Aunt Jo still had four paws and a snout. She was covered with the thick black pelt of the wolf.

The huge silverback gorilla held onto a tree, then fell to its knees. Mr. Gifford stood up, smiling. He went to his sister's side. Mom spoke quietly to Aunt Jo, trying to help her. Jake, who'd had much more practice at morphing back and forth, tried to help too. The wolf howled and shook its head.

"Easy, Jo," said Mr. Gifford. "Just relax and see yourself as human. It's easier than morphing to an animal. The wolf hung its head and teardrops glistened on its face. The fur retreated and disappeared. Aunt Jo was back. Mom hugged her.

"Good job, Mom," said Jake. He patted her on the back. I tried to smile, but my beak wouldn't curve.

The croc lay there, watching us. "Isn't that sweet," he rasped. He swiveled his head, scanning the scene. "My family, all together again to see me die."

"You aren't going to die," said Katerie. "I brought the anti-venom to the death adder's bite. If you morph back, I'll inject it."

Gramps walked forward. "Give it up, Dunn. All this happened long ago. We're old now. It's time to enjoy what we have."

The crocodile snarled at him, snapping his jagged teeth. "It's all right for you, professor. You with your fancy education and your money, lording it over me at the zoo."

"I told you the government would pay our tuition. You laughed at me. Said you had other ways of making money." He lowered his voice. "Most of them illegal."

The medicine woman pounded the ground three times with her stick. We'd all heard her threat. There were only two of us who hadn't returned to human. I couldn't, and Dunn wouldn't.

The net flattened. Through the openings in the net oozed something long and thin as a garden hose. It rolled in the dirt, growing wider and bigger until it became an enormous snake. Still growing, it reared, spreading its hood. On the back of the hood, two dark circles, one on each side of a U-shaped marking, resembled a pair of eyeglasses. Dunn had morphed into his most dangerous form: the spectacled cobra. Up, up, up went the cobra, weaving back and forth as it grew to a height of thirty feet. The gargantuan snake could produce a puddle of deadly venom, enough to kill us all in seconds.

The medicine woman watched him, her eyes wide. Did she know what she'd unleashed? Why didn't she stop him? Maybe she couldn't. She was very old and might have lost some of her powers. Katerie had turned pale, clearly helpless. Megan had fire in her eyes. She was staring at me, and I could feel her strength.

I watched the snake grow with a sinking heart. If I fought it, I would remain an eagle forever. The feathers were still not natural to me, and I hated them. I longed to be human again. To feel Mom's soft cheek as she kissed me. To play catch with Dad and Austin in the park. To eat ice cream and pizza and blueberry muffins. But I had no choice. If I didn't stop it, the cobra would kill us all.

Austin pressed close to me and whispered, "Don't do it,

Luke." He had tears in his eyes. I looked away, blinking back my own tears. "I'll come with you." His voice was hoarse.

"No." I brushed his arm with my wing. "Take care of our folks. I love you, bro."

Chapter Thirteen—One Last Thing About the Curse

A crimson glow spread across the water as the sun peeked over the horizon. The snake reared, its upper body arching from its great height. I moved behind it. The circles on the back of its hood were as big as tractor tires. Bobbing and weaving, it bent toward the terrified people below. My family. Megan's family. The cobra reared again and curved downward, cackling with laughter as it hissed and tormented them. It wasn't watching me.

Keeping my wings wrapped, I focused and supersized. Ten feet tall. Then twenty feet. I kept going until I was sure my beak was long enough to clamp down on that arrogant, deadly snake's neck. At thirty feet I stopped growing. My talons were strong, curved, and big enough to clench a cow without dropping it. My beak was deadly, six feet long, and as sharp as a saber.

Dunn was still taunting his victims. I stood on the beach, catching Megan's smile and my brother's look of hope. The cool morning breeze ruffled my neck feathers. As I lifted off, the rising sun behind me tipped my spreading wings with fire.

Up, up, up into the sky I rose. Flipping my body, I aimed for the earth.

I dove so fast the snake didn't have time to hiss. Opening my beak, I grabbed the monstrous cobra by the neck and shook it. It arched and spun its tail, sending sprays of sand in all directions. Fighting against the strength of my clamped beak, it threw itself back and forth beneath me. I bit down harder, holding it tightly as it arched and squirmed, trying to get away. Its swaying became weaker. The snake went limp. I carried it far enough from the onlookers that it couldn't hurt anyone, then dropped it in the dirt with a thud. The giant cobra deflated like a balloon, its body narrowing and shortening back to the size of an ordinary four-foot cobra. A dead or nearly dead cobra. The snake's tail stirred, then stretched and widened into the shape of a man. Dunn lay still, his eyes half open. His skin was a pasty white and his breath came in rasps.

I landed next to my brother and let myself shrink to normal eagle size. My mother wrapped her arms around me, her eyes filled with tears. Megan gently touched my wing. Austin stared at the ground, his face pale and sad. Gramps patted my feathered shoulder.

Mairghread walked slowly over to us. "It is over," she said. She raised her arms to the sky, as if she were about to gather in the stars. I wanted to ask her why Dunn had become human again and I hadn't. But what happened next made me forget my question.

Though it had been a clear morning, the sky was turning a funny shade of green. The air was damp and heavy. It felt as if something terrible was going to happen, like a bad storm or a tornado. Austin took Megan's hand and scooped me up with his other arm.

The wind began to howl. It slashed at the trees, breaking branches and hurling them through the air. Blossoms tore from trees and soared in the wind. Waves crashed onto the shore, dragging the crate out to sea. The cook and another man picked Dunn up and dragged him toward the cave, followed by the medicine woman. Her skirt, whipped by the wind, had wrapped around her body. Her long white hair blew around her face and spread against her mouth. Katerie supported her, keeping her hand under her mother's elbow.

Though the cave was large, we jammed together just inside the entrance. No one wanted to move further in, because the cave was already occupied. Lying on her belly, the pink Komodo stretched out like an old watchdog. Behind her, twenty gray Komodos lifted their heads, watching us with bright, interested eyes. Roux stood up, hissing and flicking her forked tongue. Mairghread spoke to her in a low voice. Roux settled down again, her wide body blocking the path of the gray Komodos.

Outside, horse-size waves galloped onto the shore. The wind smashed into the trees, bending the tops and breaking limbs. Coconuts and mangos thudded to the ground and rolled into the bending weeds to hide.

We huddled together in the mouth of the cave, watching the sky. Gramps had his arm around Mom. She pulled Austin and me closer to her side. My eagle head didn't even reach her waist. Austin picked me up so I could see. Mr. Gifford and Megan, Aunt Jo and Jake huddled next to us, all of us alert to signs of danger from behind or above us. Katerie stood next to her mother, her eyes wide with fear. Mairghread held her long stick, pushing it against the cave floor to keep her balance.

Tinged with silver, figures began to form in the sky. A

blurry sailor jabbed a glowing pink Komodo with a big stick. A jagged line formed in the green sky, streaking it with red.

"The hole in the Whole," whispered Austin. I nodded, still breathless and worried.

The images shaped themselves into new scenes, each one fading to give way to the next. A fisherman threw lighted sticks of dynamite into the ocean. The reef turned to fire, then into hills of dead brown coral. Fish of all sizes, sharks and an octopus floated dead across the sky. The jagged tear widened and drips of red seeped from it as if from a bleeding wound. Pictures came and went, showing scenes like the ones on the wall of the cave. Men carried Komodos upside down with their front and back legs tied together, then stuffed them into crates. Silver coins overflowed from one hand to another and fell to the ground. The rip grew so wide that the sky turned red—the hole in the Whole exploding open from greedy damage. Murky green erased the red and the pictures began again.

A boy with red hair, reading, while another reached over him to turn a page. The first boy swung his fist backwards, hitting the second boy in the nose. A wave of shame washed over me. My badness was there in the sky for all to see. I waited to see the rip in the universe get bigger, but something quite different happened.

Lightning pierced the air, forming gold rings around the boys. One became a Komodo dragon and the other became a grizzly bear. The bear lay on the cement of its cage, looking hungry and weak. The Komodo knocked over an ice cream cart and shoved treats into a bag. It carried the bag to the bear and tried to fling it into the cage. The jagged line with its huge blanket of red appeared in the sky again, but this time the tear grew smaller and some of the red disappeared. The Komodo scooped hamburgers from a counter and shoved them into a bag. Chased by zookeepers, it tried to throw the bag toward the bear. Though the bag fell short, the tear overhead grew smaller again.

We were getting the idea now. The rip in the fabric of the universe—the hole in the Whole—could change. Bad deeds made the tear wider, and good deeds seemed to mend it. A Dunn-like image appeared several times, wielding the cattle prod, stealing the red snake, putting a rattlesnake in a giant concrete egg. Each time the rip grew wider and it looked like it would never be mended again.

"Dunn has caused a lot of damage," muttered Austin.

"What is in the One is in the Whole," I whispered. "That's what the medicine woman said."

In the sky, the pictures bloomed and faded like the pages of a giant photo album. A red-haired girl turned into a red snake. A boy turned eagle and caught the red snake as it fell through the sky. A giant crocodile capsized a ship. A great turtle swam upward, a woven bracelet visible on its thick front leg. A gray cloud erased the turtle, leaving behind the shape of an elephant. The elephant waded into an ocean of turquoise and then reshaped itself into a huge dolphin. Above it, a blonde cougar faded into the sky, followed by a great gray wolf and a wild boar. Other animals appeared and dissolved: a cobra, a mongoose, a wolverine, a hyena, a rat, and a giant, awkward crocodile. A silverback gorilla and a small red snake twisted their way upward, their shapes disappearing into the clouds. A huge brown bear pummeled the atmosphere and faded. A giant lizard was drawn up to the sky, followed by a soaring eagle. Lightning shot across the dark, and the earth fell silent.

A cold wind ruffled my feathers. I turned to make sure the others were okay. Everyone was staring at the sky except Dunn Nikowski. He was huddled in a corner, staring at the medicine woman, who stood with her hand on the head of the pink Komodo. The myna bird hopped toward him and squawked, "Give us a kiss! Give us a kiss!" The cook grabbed the bird and put her back on his shoulder.

Outside, the ground began to bubble. The wind whipped up a tornado of color. Purple, orange, yellow, and green whirled into a funnel and spun from the ground to the top of the trees. Someone screamed. Austin had one arm around Megan and reached out to me with the other hand. I tried to stretch my wing to him, but I couldn't move. Everyone in the cave seemed frozen with fear. Mairghread kept her hand on Roux's head. The gray dragons behind her flicked their forked tongues and blinked at each other. The twirling colors fell to the ground, forming a tunnel outside the cave.

"Go now!" cried Mairghread. "Everyone must go through. Hurry!"

Austin and Megan stepped into the tunnel and disappeared. Mr. Gifford, Aunt Jo, and Jake went next. Gramps had Mom's hand. "Come on," he said. "Go through, Laura. Don't be afraid."

"I'm not going without Luke!" She reached for my wing and tried to pull.

"He's staying here," snarled Dunn. He was on his knees, his arms around my legs. The tunnel was closing. I kept trying to pull away.

"Go, Mom!" I cried. "I'll be right behind you."

Mairghread spoke to the pink Komodo. Roux rose and came toward Dunn. He let go of me and fell back into a heap on the floor.

"Now, Luke!" said the medicine woman. I dove into the tunnel and felt it close behind me.

The ground rocked and sizzled like a frying pan, just as it had in the zoo that fateful day last fall. Everything went dark. I was floating in a soft, warm pool.

"Wait! Let me go through!" Dunn's voice echoed into the distance.

The twirling stopped abruptly, releasing me into the atmosphere. I spread out my arms and felt hard, gritty ground beneath me. I pushed myself up. It was light again, and we were all on the beach several yards downhill from the cave.

Luke!" Megan ran to me, throwing her arms around my waist and hugging. I hugged her back. I had arms! I had a waist to hug! Her hair smelled sweet and felt soft on my cheek. I reached up and felt my mouth, my nose, and my eyes. The beak was gone.

Austin put his arms around me too. His eyes were filled with tears. So were mine. I hugged him back and felt the strong muscles of his arms and back. He no longer smelled like bear. Still a little shorter than me but twice as strong, I guessed.

"Are you guys okay?" Mom pulled us both into her arms, laughing and crying at the same time. "They're gone, Luke. All your feathers are gone."

My hands and arms were totally normal. Not a feather anywhere. My legs had no feathers either. No talons! I was wearing shoes—the same ones I'd had on when we left home. I hadn't seen them in so long I'd forgotten what they looked like. Megan's bracelet was still on my wrist, a tiny heart fastened to the place where it clipped together. I felt for my wallet. It was there in my back pocket. I opened it and saw my small stash of money. My pocketknife and small flashlight were in the other pocket.

Austin examined his arms. "No fur!" he exclaimed. "Just skin." His face beamed with joy. "It's good to see you, bro!"

"Are you okay? Do you hurt where they jabbed you with the cattle prod?"

Austin shook his head. "I'm fine."

"Me too." I grinned at him.

Gramps was sitting on the ground, his face in his hands. His shoulders were shaking. I went over and sat down next to him.

"It's okay, Gramps," I said softly. "I'm human again, and we're all okay."

He raised his face and wiped the tears from his cheeks with his sleeve. "I should have stayed, Luke. I should have stayed behind and helped undo the curse. Then none of this suffering would ever have happened to any of you. But I didn't believe it."

"Who *would* believe it? Besides, you would have been court-martialed for going AWOL, right? Then you would have been in the brig and couldn't have helped anyone. And it turned out okay."

"Yes." He pulled a handkerchief from his pocket, wiped his eyes again, and smiled. "Good to see you again, Luke. I have to admit I was worried."

"Dunn caused all this trouble. He should at least be punished for trying to steal a Komodo," I said.

"He will be," said Gramps. "I called the police before we came down the hill. They should be getting here any minute." He took a deep breath. "He probably isn't going to live very long."

I let out a long breath. "I tried not to kill him."

Gramps nodded. "I know. You did what you had to do. But he still has death adder venom in his system."

Megan ran to us. She grinned and twirled for us. 'I'm human too," she cried.

"You always were, Megan," I said. "I mean, you didn't have any trace of your animal forms when you were human."

Megan shrugged. "Except for wanting to bite people who made me angry."

We laughed.

Everything around me seemed wonderful. The scent of flowers filled the air. I'd missed the touch of Mom's gentle hands and the strength of Austin's hugs. I was really hungry, and thirsty too. When we got back to the houseboat, I was going to have a sandwich and a soda. It was great to be human again!

And then the medicine woman was there again, leaning on her daughter's arm. I hadn't seen her emerge from the cave. When Mairghread saw me, she smiled. It was the first time she and Katerie had seen me human.

"You have kept your word," said Mairghread. "You, your brother, and my great-granddaughter have protected the pink Komodo and her eggs. The curse has been removed from all of you."

"No!" screamed Dunn. He staggered down the hill toward us.

The medicine woman raised her stick and stared at him. "Because you married my daughter, I gave you the strength of five animals. You did not use your powers to protect the Komodos and my island. Instead you used your animal powers for evil. You must pay for your damage to the great Whole. You and your friends will go to prison. Then you will be banished from the island forever."

She walked to the cook, who still had the myna bird on his shoulder. The medicine woman held out her finger, and the myna bird stepped onto it. "You are not to blame for any of this," she said to the myna. "You may choose to go or stay, whatever you wish."

"Give us a kiss," said the myna. Then she stepped back to the cook's shoulder. Maggie was going to stay with Mr. Burnell. I hoped she knew she was about to be arrested.

"Press your bracelets together," said medicine woman. "Let the pink Komodo hear the song."

Austin, Megan, and I held our wrists together. From somewhere above us, we heard the tinkling of tiny bells. Roux waddled slowly out of the cave. She headed down the hill toward us, her long scaly tail brushing the dirt. Something glittered on the end of her tail. I squinted, trying to see it.

"It's a little star," whispered Megan. "I saw it before but I thought it had to be my imagination."

"It's just the way the sun hits the scales," said Austin.

The Komodo plodded along, finally stopping in front of Mairghread. She raised her snout, looking at the medicine woman as though waiting for the next instruction. Mairghread reached into her pocket and brought out a small fish. She tossed it to the Komodo, who caught it on the fly.

The medicine woman turned to us. "I taught her to do that. She comes when she hears the sound of the bells."

"You said if we didn't change form back to human, we would stay in our animal form forever. But I didn't. Thank you," I said. "Thank you so much."

Mairghread shrugged. "You didn't change from your eagle form so you could do what I asked—help to heal the hole in the Whole." She smiled at me. "I realized I'd been mistaken too. I'd given Dunn exactly what he wanted. He wanted the animal forms and the power they brought him. All you wanted was to be human again. It wasn't fair."

Turning, she looked at each of us; then her gaze rested on Katerie. "Roux and I are leaving now, my dearest," she said. "We are both very old, and it is time for us to rest."

Katerie rushed to her mother, crying out. Mairghread put her arms around her daughter and held her close.

"I knew this day would come," sobbed Katerie, "but I'm not ready. Please don't leave."

"I won't be far away," said the medicine woman. "You have only to feel me in your heart and you can talk to me." Katerie nodded. Tears ran down her cheeks as her mother kissed her and hugged her again.

My eyes were filling with tears too. I couldn't bear to lose Mom. Poor Katerie. It didn't seem to make any difference that her mother was old. She didn't want to lose her mom either.

Mairghread brushed the hair away from Megan's eyes and kissed her on the forehead. She stroked Megan's cheek. "You look just like my granddaughter, Angelina."

Megan blinked, nodding. "My mother," she whispered. Then she wiped her eyes with her sleeve.

The medicine woman lifted her chin and straightened her shoulders. "Come," she said, waving to Roux. A tiny bell began to tinkle. Megan and Austin looked at their bracelets. They hadn't pressed them together. The medicine woman nodded to us. "Well done, my young friends. When I am gone,

Katerie will give you something I've left for you."

We stood together, holding hands, watching them go up the hill. The medicine woman walked slowly, as though she carried the burdens of the world on her back. Roux waddled along after her, dragging her long pink tail. A silver star twinkled at us from the tail's end. Mom and Gramps put their arms around me and Austin. Megan moved next to Katerie and held her grandmother's hand. Jake and Mr. Gifford stood on each side of Aunt Jo. No one spoke as we watched Mairghread and the pink Komodo climb the hill, walking farther and farther away from us. Even the air around us seemed still, as though something sacred was going to happen.

When they reached the top, Mairghread turned and lifted her hand. Megan and Katerie raised their hands. The medicine woman turned back to Roux, placing her hand on the dragon's head. I blinked, and they were gone.

I wanted to run up the hill, to take another look at them. If I flew, I could be there in seconds. But I couldn't fly anymore.

A shiver went down my back. Something was wrong. Someone was missing from the group. Dunn! Then I saw him, several yards away, reeling like a drunk. His skin was ashen.

"You think you've won, but you haven't," he croaked. His voice was so hoarse we could barely understand him. "The pink Komodo is gone. Only these are left! But not for long!" He held up a bulging cloth bag. His arm shook as though it was too heavy for him to hold. "You will never return a pink Komodo to the people of Komodo Island!"

"The eggs!" I yelled. "He's got the eggs!"

"Grandfather! Please! Stop!" Megan took off in soccer-star style, heading for Dunn.

Austin took off after Megan. "Megan, stay away from him," he shouted. "I'll get the eggs."

Dunn moved like a damaged robot, each metal leg jarring his body. He was about fifty yards from the shore, where whitecaps washed over jagged boulders. If he threw that bag on the rocks, all the eggs would be broken. If they tackled him, he'd fall on the eggs and break them that way.

"The rope!" I yelled.

Mom flung the rope toward me. I caught it and quickly made several coils that I took in my left hand. Running, I tried to head Dunn off as he zigzagged toward the rocky shore. If I could stop him without knocking him down, and get the rope over him so his arms were pinned to his sides, that would prevent him from throwing the bag.

Taking the loop in my right hand, I began to swing it over my head. Dunn staggered back toward me, with Austin and Megan on each side of him, herding him in my direction. Both were trying to talk him into handing over the bag. They were also buying time for me to get closer. I let the loop fly just as Dunn started to raise his arm. My heart thudded as the loop soared lightly through the air. It landed neatly over Dunn's shoulders just an instant after he tossed the bag into the air. Jake, coming out of nowhere, grabbed Dunn's legs at the same time. Dunn hit the ground, empty-handed.

The bag arced into the sky and began to drop. Megan, still running, had her arms open and her eyes on the bag. Not watching the ground, she reached for the bag as it plummeted toward the earth, then tripped and fell backwards, landing with a thump. It was the kind of catch that would be shown over and over on the sports networks if it had happened in front of a camera. We hurried to her side. Megan lay on the sand less than a yard from the rocks, the bag lightly cradled to her chest. Austin and I knelt next to her and helped her sit up. Beads of sweat bloomed on her forehead and cheeks. Taking a shuddering breath, she handed me the bag. I opened it carefully and we all looked in. Seven eggs, all still intact. Austin pulled Megan to her feet. "Nice work, medicine girl," he said, grinning.

I clapped Jake on the back. "That was great, Jake. You'd have gotten him if the rope missed." I didn't tell Jake that Austin hadn't taken Dunn down because he probably would have fallen on the bag and broken all the eggs. Our goal was to make him stop running and keep him from tossing the bag. But I wanted to make Jake feel like he'd done something good. He'd tried to help. That was new behavior for him, and he was doing his best.

Jake beamed. "Guess we make a good team."

Chapter Fourteen—The Last Task

We were sitting together beneath a mango tree, resting from the long day and an even longer night. Gramps had gotten us tickets for a flight out of a small airport on a nearby island. The adults had gone to the houseboat to sleep for a couple of hours before Captain Miklos came to take us to the island where the airport was located. Jake had taken the panda back to the rangers' station to feed her and give her water. A ship was coming to get her and take her back to China, but we didn't know when it would arrive. Katerie and the villagers would take care of her until then. They would also see that she had plenty of bamboo shoots so she wouldn't be hungry on the trip home.

Austin, Megan, and I had one last task to accomplish. We had fulfilled our promise and protected Roux and her eggs. Mairghread had removed the curse, and all of our animal traits were gone. But the old pink Komodo was gone now, and there were no more on the island. The original curse said a pink Komodo had to be returned to the people of the island. Mairghread hadn't held us to it, but I wasn't taking any chances. I wanted to make sure the people had another pink Komodo before we left. Roux's eggs were my last hope.

The bag sat in the grass next to us, the sides pulled down so we could watch the eggs for any kind of movement.

"What if they don't hatch before we leave?" asked Megan.

"Your grandmother will write and tell you, and you can tell us," said Austin.

I leaned back against the tree and stared out at the water. It was beautiful here. This was the first time I'd seen it as a human. In my eagle form, I was too miserable to care. Austin leaned back against the tree too, closing his eyes.

Megan's voice pierced through the fog of tiredness that enclosed us. "Look, they're cracking!"

One egg wobbled back and forth, a long vertical crack splitting and lifting a piece of the shell. The rest of the shell swelled and collapsed as though it was breathing. A striped snout broke through; then we saw tiny eyes covered with something clear and gray. It stayed like that, not coming out or retreating. After about a minute, part of the neck slithered through, so it looked like a snake was hatching. The coloring was yellow green and black, camouflage that would hide it in the trees and keep it from being eaten by the larger Komodos. One more burst of energy and the upper shoulders were out, showing yellow markings on the gray skin. A fully formed, seven-inch-long body, with gray, green, and yellow patches, wobbled out of the egg and onto the sand. A new baby Komodo had just been born.

We made ourselves comfortable, saying nothing. My heart was too full, and I guessed the others felt the same way. Two more eggs had also split open, and little heads were popping out. I felt the first shock of disappointment. These were the only eggs left from a pink Komodo. So far three had hatched, and the babies were all gray. What if none of them was pink?

Four more to go. Megan's face was sad, and I knew she was thinking the same thing. Still, the eggs were safe and we could guard the hatchlings until they made it to the trees. That would fulfill our promise to the medicine woman.

I took Megan's hand. "We did what we came here to do," I whispered. "The pink Komodo must have been an anomaly. They probably aren't supposed to exist."

Megan dabbed at her cheeks. I rubbed my eyes with the back of my hand to blot the tears. It seemed like my heart was overflowing with love for the two people beside me and the wondrous thing we were watching. Because a new creature was emerging from the fourth shell now—peeking out, cracking through, and then standing shakily upright with a piece of shell stuck to its gloriously pink head.

"There it is!" I cried.

"It's pink!" said Austin and Megan together.

"Don't let it get away! We have to get it back to the people of Komodo Island!" Even as I spoke, fear gripped my heart. We had to protect these babies, and especially the pink one. We had to get them somewhere safe. Where? How?

"Look!" cried Megan. "Another one!"

The next baby shoved its fragile cover sideways, leaving a strand of slime still connected to a stubby pink leg. I gulped, overwhelmed and grateful. There were two brand new baby pink Komodos!

"Two more left." Austin's voice sounded thrilled and hopeful. There were seven eggs. So far we had two pink babies and three gray ones. Even the gray-green ones would be precious to the islanders, because they were the hatchlings of their beloved Roux. The next egg split and a gray-green leg shoved through. The baby scrambled out, mouth open and sharp baby teeth ready for food. The last egg rocked back and forth, then rolled over. The hatchling butted its way through the shell and marched proudly out, dragging its scaly pink tail. On the end of the tail was a tiny star.

Megan stared at it, eyes wide. She blinked and blinked again. "Do you see what I see?" she asked.

"It's just a reflection from the sun," said Austin. But he was smiling.

We watched them crawl around, poking their heads in the air, their tiny eyes bright and already frightening.

"Don't let them bite you," I warned. "They're already venomous."

"Where can we put them?" asked Megan.

"If we weren't here, they'd head for a tree. Let's take them to the village, to Katerie and the Elder, and then let them go up into a tree near Katerie's hut. The villagers can decide what to do with them from there."

"That fulfills our last task," said Austin.

"Returning a pink Komodo to the people of Komodo Island," added Megan.

"We did better than that," I said, feeling proud. "We're taking them three!"

The little reptiles started to walk, heading for the tree we were leaning against.

"Don't let them get away!" I exclaimed. "I'll get a box from the houseboat."

It took me a few minutes to find a box. When I got back

to the tree, Megan was playing with one of the pink babies. As she walked in a circle, the little Komodo followed her. Then Megan turned and pointed down at it. "Asta, stay!" she said firmly. She backed up a step. The pink hatchling stood still, looking up at her with beady little eyes. Megan glanced at me and grinned. She reached down and fed the little Komodo a bug. The baby snapped it up with tiny, razor-sharp teeth, then looked up at her, mouth open. When it wiggled its scaly pink tail, I saw the tiny star on the end.

"What did you call the baby?" I asked.

"Asta," said Megan. "It means 'star.' Isn't that a perfect name?"

Austin's eyes met mine. He took a deep breath, and I could sense his thoughts. They were the same as mine. Megan was becoming more like her great-grandmother every minute. We had to get her off this island. Fast.

Wearing Mom's oven gloves, I picked up the babies and placed them in the box. They twisted and snapped at my hand, looking for food. We took the seven hatchlings to Katerie, who was cooking outside her hut. She smiled and hugged all three of us, and then called to the others to come and see the new arrivals. Soon the villagers had crowded around us, laughing and talking. They took turns looking in the box, pointing with amazement at the three pink hatchlings.

"Three pink ones! Think of that. And did you see the star on that one's tail?" asked Katerie. "Just like the mother."

When everyone had seen them, we put them on the ground near the tree.

"Tree!" said Megan. The pink baby with the silver star on its tail began waddling toward the tree. The others followed along behind it.

"Great," muttered Austin. "Medicine girl speaks and all of nature obeys." He clapped his hand across his eyes and shook his head. "Will someone please give me a ticket back to reality?"

I shivered all over, hoping I hadn't just seen a sign of the future.

When all the babies had climbed into the tree, Austin leaned back against the trunk. "What will they eat up there?" he asked, staring up into the branches.

"Eggs, bugs, lizards, or any little mammal that is dumb enough to crawl up there, I guess." The lady ranger would know. Megan would ask her about that and a lot more. She'd probably ask for a weekly report to be emailed to her at home.

***

The feast was ready. Everyone had gathered together in the center of the village. Mom, Gramps, Aunt Jo, Mr. Gifford, and Jake were seated at a table. The three of us sat down with them. Katerie stepped forward with a narrow box in her hand. She asked Austin and me to come forward.

"Before my mother left, she asked me to give you a special honor," said Katerie. She reached into the box and took out a small golden feather on a golden chain. She hung the chain around my neck. "This golden feather is for the vision and valor you have shown," she said. "It will connect you with us always." She placed a golden chain over Austin's head. From it hung a golden claw. "This golden claw is for the strength and integrity you have shown," she said. "It will connect you with us always."

Then Katerie asked Megan to come and stand next to her. Megan was wearing a long flowered skirt that looked similar to her grandmother's. The shell pendant no longer glowed pink when I was near. I felt a little sad about that, though I didn't know why.

Katerie handed Megan two beads. "The first is for wisdom that has come down from the medicine women in our history," said Katerie. "The second bead is for trust in your destiny. Both of these beads will connect you with us always." She helped Megan put the beads on the necklace with the shell pendant. The wisdom bead was pink with silver strands around it. The bead for trust sparkled like gray glass. Looking at them made me shiver again as I wondered what Megan's future would be.

"I have one more gift to give," said Katerie. "Jake, would you come forward?"

Jake frowned worriedly as he glanced at me. I shrugged and shook my head. I didn't have a clue what was going on either.

Jake walked awkwardly to Katerie's side and stood shuffling from one foot to the other. Katerie put a hand on his arm and he went still. She seemed to have a calming effect on him.

"You have found a new path," said Katerie. "Sailors use the stars sometimes to find their way. This silver starfish is for you. It will connect you with us always." She placed a chain with the silver starfish over his head. Jake's face turned red, but he looked pleased. Everyone clapped, and then we settled down to eat. It was the first feast I had eaten since returning human, and the roast pork tasted delicious.

After we were finished eating, Austin and I went to the rangers' station to pack up the few things we'd gathered on the island. Soon we would be on our way home. I let out a long breath. The heaviness in my chest was gone. I glanced at my arms and legs, just to make sure. No feathers. No talons. I felt my head. Hair. The wind blew through it, lifting it off my neck. My neck? Yikes! I needed a haircut.

Gramps came to fetch us. Captain Miklos was here, and it was time to board the boat. Jake sat a little distance away, staring at the panda. She looked fat and glossy, far healthier than she'd been when we arrived. He'd left a haystack-sized pile of bamboo shoots just outside the door and had taught some village children how to feed the panda and clean the shed.

"What will happen to her?" he asked, worry mixed with his sadness.

"Maddie contacted an organization that protects wild animals and the environment," said Gramps. "They've agreed to give her a ride back to China on their ship. They'll also keep an eye on the island. The fishermen have caused permanent damage to the ecosystem with their bombs. Also, Dunn and his group aren't the only ones who have tried to steal Komodo dragons. Theft of the dragons has become a major problem. They might have to close down the island to protect the remaining ones."

Dunn and five other men had been arrested earlier. Three of the crew, including Mr. Burnell, had been handcuffed and led onto the officers' ship. Dunn, who had collapsed, was taken on board on a litter carried by two men. Two villagers were also arrested. When the police boat pulled away, I felt a huge weight lifted from my mind. Dunn was gone.

Gramps told us that Captain Miklos would take us to Labuan Bajo, where we would catch a plane to Jakarta, then on from there. We had a long way to go, but every part of the trip would take us closer to home. We'd be there in about two days. I was so tired I thought I'd probably sleep the whole way.

Maddie walked with us to the pier. Megan was still asking her questions. What was she going to do with her research? How old did you have to be to volunteer on Komodo Island?

"I'd love to come back here," said Megan.

"You can come here and volunteer when you're eighteen," said Maddie. "Or younger if a parent comes with you."

"Really?" A radiant smile lit up Megan's face.

Maddie grinned at her. "Really."

Megan looked at Mr. Gifford. "Did you hear that, Uncle Roy? I can volunteer here next summer if a parent comes with me." Her uncle did not look enthused. "Maddie will be here next summer too," added Megan.

Mr. Gifford and Maddie smiled at each other. "Well now, that's different," said Mr. Gifford. "Perhaps we'll both volunteer."

Austin kicked at a stone. He walked a short distance away from the group and gestured for me to come with him.

"She's going to be a freakin' ranger," he said. "She'll probably work here. And not a decent restaurant on the island. *Nothing* on the island. Not even a respectable house with air conditioning. Not even wi-fi."

"There's wi-fi in the Rangers' Station, isn't there?" Actually, I didn't really think there was, but Austin sounded so discouraged I wanted to say something hopeful.

My brother stood with his arms crossed, staring at the toes of his dusty shoes. They hadn't been shined the whole trip. He looked haggard, too, as though the trip had been too much for him. It probably had. He'd run out of Snickers bars and hadn't had a good cup of coffee since we left the big ship. Austin liked stuff like lobster, peppermint mochas, and fancy decaf tea. They hadn't served anything like that on the freighter and certainly not on the island. Here we didn't recognize most of the food we ate. Austin was barely tolerating all this. He was on the edge of sanity. If a worm crawled over his shoe, he'd probably throw himself into the ocean. But now he couldn't go dolphin.

"You don't look good, bro. You look kind of sad," I said.

He glanced up at me and then back at the ground. "You don't look too good either. But at least you don't have feathers anymore. That beak was pretty wicked looking. Not good for kissing."

Austin took a deep breath. He held out his hand as if to shake mine. "You win, Luke."

I stared at his hand. "What are you talking about? What have I won?"

He turned away from me, and his voice sounded hoarse. "I can see it all now. You'll be a freakin' ranger too, and probably work it so you're assigned here. Megan will be right behind you, both of you in those ugly khaki uniforms. Sooner or later you'll turn around and notice her. You'll love her as much as she loves you. You'll spend your lives together, here among the dragons. Or maybe you'll both ride off into the sunset somewhere and that will be that. So, as I said, you win."

I stared at him, speechless. Austin had left reality and was now orbiting around Planet Lunacy. This was ridiculous. I had to straighten him out before his thoughts got any crazier.

"We aren't playing poker, Austin. You can't win or lose a girl like she's a teddy bear in one of those tents at the fair. Besides, I keep telling you, I'm not looking for a girlfriend." I clapped him on the back. "I'm just starting high school, Austin. Just starting! You don't even start high school for two more years. After that we'll all go to college. I'll go in four years, and you and Megan will go in six. A lot of things could change in that time." I glanced around to make sure no one was listening to this insane conversation. "Besides, Megan might totally change her mind and decide to be a pediatrician or something."

Austin's shoulders slumped again. "Great. That adds another eight years of school."

Our group was boarding Captain Miklos's boat. Gramps was waving for us to come. I gave him the "just a minute" signal. My little brother needed some frank advice, and I didn't want to embarrass him by having everybody else hear it.

"Austin, you aren't old enough to date yet. Neither is Megan. Neither am I, and I'm almost three years older than you." I let that sink in for a couple of seconds, and then continued. "Right now all you need to worry about is helping us get home. You can figure out your life plan tomorrow. You might want to get Megan's input if you're including her. Don't be surprised if she thinks you're nuts. She'll be busy planning for the fall term and what language she's going to take and which sports she's going to play. That's what you should be doing too."

Austin brightened. "Think Mom will let me play football this year?"

"Sure!" I said cheerfully. The truth was, Mom would never give her consent. She wouldn't risk his brilliant brain getting concussed. But I liked seeing him smile again. He could face the truth later, when he had Snickers bars and the latest *Wall Street Journal* in his backpack.

Chapter Fifteen—Epilogue

The islands grew smaller and smaller until all I could see were tiny shapes in an ocean of blue.

"Does it look different to you now?" asked my mother. I'd forgotten she was sitting across the aisle from me on the plane.

"It's beautiful. It's hard to believe this was all real." Mom had her compact out, powdering her nose with the little flat sponge thing that comes with it.

"Could I use that mirror for a minute?" Mom smiled as she handed it to me. I opened it up and looked at myself. Red hair, ordinary looking face. No feathers, no scales, nothing but normal human-being skin. Breathing a sigh of relief, I handed the compact back to Mom.

Austin and Megan were in the seats behind me, talking about some teacher they'd had in advanced math class. It felt good to listen and not understand a thing they were talking about. A flight attendant rolled her cart down the aisle, offering drinks and snacks. I had a soda with lots of ice and two bags of pretzels. We'd be getting dinner on the next flight. And a movie!

I woke up when we landed at Los Angeles International. A couple of hours later we boarded a plane that would take us to Chicago. When we were on the last leg of the trip, I had borrowed Mom's phone to call my friend Jim. He answered, sounding just like he had at camp. I'd been halfway around the world in the past three weeks, but it felt as if I'd just seen him yesterday.

"We just left Chicago," I said. "We'll be home in an hour. Let's get some kids together and go to a movie this weekend."

"No feathers?" asked Jim.

"Not on me. They gave me a golden feather, though, to say thank you."

Jim chuckled. "So I take it you're flying *inside* the plane."

"Yep. The stewardess is handing out pretzels and sodas right now. Mom says I have to hang up because calls from a plane are expensive. I just wanted to say hi. I'll call you tomorrow. Bye, Jim."

It was almost nine by the time we got to Detroit. Dad was waiting for us in Baggage Claim. When he saw us, a huge grin spread across his face. He gave me a big hug and said he'd missed me. I'd missed him too. I couldn't wait to get home. I would take a shower and let the nice hot water run into my hair and over my skin. Maybe we'd all hunker down in front of the television with a big bowl of popcorn and watch one of our favorite movies together. I would sleep in my clean, comfortable bed and know Austin was safe in his bed with the soft topper and the special pillow that he loved. Maybe he'd have a cup of Court Lodge decaf first.

Back in my room, I opened my new backpack and took out the chain with the little golden feather Katerie had given me. She'd told me the feather would help me if I ever needed it. I hoped I wouldn't need it. Closing my eyes, I thought about how it felt to feel the wind under my wings and glide along high in the sky. It was almost as if I could feel myself flying and see the earth far below me. I opened my eyes. I was still in my room, in my house, with my feet on the floor. I'd loved being able to see so far and soar high in the air, but I would much rather be human—one hundred percent human.

Climbing into bed, I settled back on the crisp, clean sheets. Lying on my bed was so much more comfortable than being perched on a mat somewhere. My pillow smelled nice from the stuff Mom used when she did the wash. I'd be learning all about that soon, because Mom said it was time that Austin and I learned to do our own laundry. We couldn't argue with her. She was right. We'd both aged a couple of years in the last three weeks. We'd seen another part of the world. We'd learned how to defend ourselves and others in many forms. We had faced difficult challenges and gotten through them by working together and helping each other. We'd learned that evil will eventually be defeated, and that good people working together could stop those who tried to destroy the natural world to get power and money. We'd learned that, with the right kind of kindness and support, bad people could sometimes change.

It was so good to be home. We could play games on our cellphones and drink sodas and eat tacos or hamburgers or ice cream. Austin could go back to thrilling the Lacrosse coach, and I could practice for track. For some reason, I was still pretty fast. School would be starting next week, and there was a lot to do to get ready. Austin and I had gotten new backpacks at one of those airport shops, but we still had to get our books and school supplies. We both needed new clothes—longer pants and bigger shoes and school sweatshirts. We wanted to get some new short-sleeved shirts too. I didn't have to cover up any feathers, and Austin didn't have any fur. Both of us were glad to look ordinary and not stand out.

We could move forward into the future with confidence. All we had to do now was get through high school, then college, and then find a job somewhere. Compared with what we'd been through, that all sounded pretty easy to me. Megan would be with her Uncle Roy and Aunt Jo, who was going to stay with them. Aunt Jo was going to ask for custody of Jake, since he wanted to live with her. Gramps thought the judge would probably okay the arrangement. So Megan had gone from having only one relative to having a big family. She and Jake had talked a lot on the plane and seemed to be getting closer.

Gramps wasn't going to mention anything to the judge about what had happened on the ship. Jake had morphed into a form he couldn't control, and it wasn't his fault that he could morph in the first place. It was like letting a kid steer a rocket when he hadn't even learned how to drive a car.

Austin had grown during the summer, and now he was only a couple of inches shorter than me. Maybe he'd even grow taller than me. I didn't care how much taller, stronger, or smarter he was, just so he was home and safe. We had a few more years together before I went to college. I'd go to all his games and cheer him on. I'd cheer him on in whatever he did, for the rest of our lives. He'd be there for me, too.

And Megan? She was going to go to college, probably somewhere far away. She'd written down Maddie's address and phone number, and was planning to stay in touch. She could go to Komodo Island as a volunteer as soon as she was old enough. It wouldn't surprise me if she went back to see Katerie next summer. Would she stay there and become their medicine woman someday? I'd asked her that on the way home. Megan had laughed and said, "Be their medicine woman? Only if I go to med school first."

I checked myself in the mirror again, close up. Same red hair, same ordinary face. No beak. No eagle feathers anywhere. I was completely, totally human. I was completely, totally grateful—for that and so much more in my life.

I took the golden feather from its box and hung the chain from my mirror, where I could see it. That adventure was over. We were all safely back home, and together. Tomorrow we would have bacon, eggs, and blueberry muffins for breakfast. Life was really, really good!

The End

About The Author

M.C. (Peg) Berkhousen wrote her first poem in sixth grade and has been writing all her life. She was raised in Three Rivers, Michigan, where she frequently visited the library and checked out Cherry Ames and Sue Barton nursing stories.

After graduation from Borgess School of Nursing in Kalamazoo, Michigan, Peg integrated writing with her nursing career. She won Michigan Nurse Writer of the Year for her article on using journalism therapy with a psychiatric patient who was aboard the USS Hornet when it was sunk by the Japanese during WWII. While working in Staff Development at St.

Joseph Mercy Hospital, Pontiac, Michigan, she wrote, produced and directed staff training videos that were published by J.B. Lippincott, New York. She wrote the script and was Associate Producer for "Lincoln... In His Own Words," a project for Lincoln Life Insurance Company, narrated by actor Hal Holbrook. On faculty for Trinity International Health Services, Peg provided management training and consultation to Franciscan Sisters at Matre Dei Hospital, Bulawayo, Zimbabwe. She ended her nursing career as Director of Clinical Services, Trinity Home Health and Hospice Services.

Return to Komodo Island is the third book of the Komodo Trilogy, targeted to children in grades 5th through 8th. The first book, *Curse of the Komodo*, and the second, *90% Human*, have both won the "Story Monsters Approved" award from Story Monsters Ink magazine, a literary resource for librarians, teachers and parents. Both books also won Honorable Mentions in the 2019 Dragonfly Book Awards Contest, sponsored by Story Monsters Ink.

Like some of her readers, Peg isn't quite ready to let these characters go, and is thinking about turning the trilogy into a series. Watch her website and Author page for updates. Peg resides in Ottawa Hills, Ohio.

Progressive Rising Phoenix Press is an independent publisher. We offer wholesale discounts and multiple binding options with no minimum purchases for schools, libraries, book clubs, and retail vendors. We also offer rewards for libraries, schools, independent book stores, and book clubs. Please visit our website to see our updated catalogue of titles and our wholesale discount page at:
www.ProgressiveRisingPhoenix.com